WELL #9

WELL #9

SCOTT ROBERTS

atmosphere press

Published by Atmosphere Press

Cover design by Senhor Tocas

Well #9
2021, Scott Roberts

atmospherepress.com

For my family

AUTHOR'S NOTE

I am not an historian. I am a fiction writer, if there is such an animal. But every fiction, if it is to be believed and realistic and related to, must be rooted in a compelling truth.

The story of Patridge Raleigh, the true story of names, faces, and families, needs to be told by a journalist, historian, and scholar, and I am none of these.

However, in order for the reader to fully understand and appreciate what occurred here, it is important that you know what happened.

What happened in the Patridge Raleigh Oilfields is another example of the sacrifices we make as a society in order to go about our modern lives.

Behind every light switch is a coal miner.

Inside every car engine is a mud logger and roustabout.

The list of lambs goes on and on, and we need to acknowledge it and respect it.

In the end, respect and value is what makes a worker truly essential.

Scott Roberts 2020
Hattiesburg
via Sandy Hook, MS

PROLOGUE AND INTRODUCTION

THE TRAGEDY AT PARTRIDGE RALEIGH
JUNE 5, 2006

A BRIEF DESCRIPTION AND COMMENT

The Raleigh Oil Field was, and continues to operate, under various owners since oil was discovered there. Technologies of oil drilling and extraction have made it possible for wells that had been "played out" to be brought back online. It was precisely this that brought four workers from Stringer's Oilfield Service, based in Columbia, MS. to the Raleigh Oilfield and Well #9.

Based on information investigators with the Chemical Safety Board were able to obtain, the job for that day was to attach a new pipe to extend from a supply well to a storage well. A hatch door was opened in the supply well to allow for flammable vapors to dissipate. To test for any residual vapors, the welder on sight took a cutting torch and "flashed the tank." A vapor/gas detection meter could have been used to make a more accurate test; however, the workers were not provided with this by the company. This could have been done for a few hundred dollars, but it likely would not have prevented the accident.

Attached to the storage well was another pipe, open and pointed in the direction of the men as they worked. The storage well was connected to a twin storage well next to it. Unknown to the workers, both of these storage wells had a skim of various flammable hydrocarbons. In order to supervise the work, the foreman stood atop the supply well. The welder tethered himself to the supply well and was positioned on a ladder that had been stretched between there and the storage well. In order to keep the ladder from falling, the two other workers stood as a counterweight on the other end.

Barely a small tack weld had been made before the sparks and the flammable gas met one another, causing the tanks to catch fire. The tops of both storage tanks were blown off, killing the foreman and the two young workers on the ladder. The welder, the only survivor, was an experienced man with over thirty years as a master craftsman. He sustained major physical injuries and was only saved because he had tethered himself to the supply well.

No one can say for sure what the true cause of this tragedy is. In fact, there are many causes ranging from outright negligence of safety brought on by a rushing company driven by profits, to an over familiarity with dangerous work, to the hot Mississippi sun. In short, what we should be discussing is the fact that there are four men of various backgrounds and ages and all of their collective families and communities that have been adversely affected. Today, those two young workers would be in middle age, celebrating kindergarten graduations and birthdays of children, of nieces and nephews. The foreman and welder would be quietly retired, chasing grand-children through damp Southern Mississippi grass, or fishing in the Pearl River.

But they are not. So, we must remember them.

Something that fascinated me about this tragedy at the Raleigh Oil Fields was how quickly it seemed to be dismissed like so many other tragedies we must overcome on what seems to be a brisk, daily basis. What I saw as I researched the accident and reached out to some family members, both timidly and with a solemn respect for their privacy, was that these people were, and are, real, and the working class they represent, whether the world wants to recognize it or not, are real. Every time we enjoy some modern convenience, as we pass over the money in cash or through some cryptocurrency, we are not only paying people to risk their lives, we are becoming connected to them and the work that they do, whether we understand the work and the people or not.

As stated before, I am not an historian or a journalist. I'll leave that to people with greater attention spans. I am a fiction writer, and in keeping with that, what follows, except for the details of the accident, are fiction. The characters are not meant to represent anyone in real life. Similarities to any real people are only a coincidence of humanity and should be disregarded completely.

To my knowledge, no one named Molly or Kay or Molly Kay have ever worked for, contracted with, or otherwise been employed by the government watchdog company, The Chemical Safety Board, or CSB. I would, however, like to thank the employees of this underfunded company for their help in searching for answers as to what happened at Partridge Raleigh, as well as their written analyses that provide lay people with necessary and simple facts that can be used to avoid future disasters.

A link to the CSB website and a more in-depth description of the accident.

https://www.csb.gov/partridge-raleigh-oilfield-explosion-and-fire/

FOUR DAYS LATER

Molly Kay came out late in the afternoon. The woods were fully awake with the high pitched chirping of cicadas and squirrels and wrens rustling in the leaves, and as a gentle, sudden wind blew, the vines from above her bumped together with the tree tops in a muffled, more dull and round than clicking sound, not sharp like the cicada. Together, for a moment, she was amazed at how loud this place, all these places, could be, and no one there to hear them. She thought about the whole tree falling in the woods paradox she had heard so many times and thought to herself that no one could ignore this, present or not. Her white truck was smudged with dirt and mud from being out in the field for over a week. She had been in Hutchinson, Missouri outside of St. Louis to investigate a fire at a fertilizer plant, then Two Bridges, Kentucky, documenting, taking pictures and notes and interviewing residents after a methane gas leak from a railroad car had sent several people to the hospital. CSB was barely legible on the outside of the aged white truck. She was new, so she got the oldest truck and the far off assignments. This *Mississippi Sun* and the caldron of water it heated made her breath heavy as it entered her throat and lungs. It couldn't be the same Sun from Pennsylvania or New York or Iowa. It was different, alive, a spurned thing hurling out its revenge. The first thing she noticed when she got out and put a boot on the ground was the way the underbrush was disturbed. She uncapped the lens of her camera and clicked several times. It reminded her of what the land looks like after a logging crew finishes their work, everything in chaos, fresh dirt overturned from where the fire trucks had squeezed between the trees and spun tires in the fertile, sandy topsoil. The smells of fresh earth and the injured, slashed pine tops made her breathe deeper and to somehow enjoy it, and she enjoyed and appreciated the solemnity of the moment as she walked the small road that led to the site. Some of the trees bore the marks still. Slashes in the bark had begun to turn a dark brown and black. Her feet made the transition, where the woods had been cut out, from the sandy topsoil to the red clay rocks, hot rocks beneath her. Even in the morning it was a humid, sweltering heat that she could feel rising up to her hands and camera. She began to take pictures of the tanks and the ground and the folded piece of circular metal, the top of one of the tanks, bent like a coffee filter in the hands of a child. There was still a shirt hanging in the tree branches one hundred or more feet above.

THE MORNING OF

CHAPTER 1

LaVoy, barefoot, hair wet from the shower, his face slick and clean from his shave, walked toward the kitchen, toward the smells of bacon and coffee that had wound and slinked their way to him as he had put on his pants and shirt in the bedroom, picking it all up from a tan, cushioned chair he had laid them out on the night before. Pretty soon, he wouldn't have to anymore. He could sleep as late as he wanted and go to bed when he wanted and do *whatever* he wanted. Maybe plant a garden and see it through, make sure it stayed watered and weeded and fed with manure or fertilizer. He could choose those things too. He told his wife so as he walked into the kitchen that morning.

Smiling, she said, "You better retire so you can *fix this house*. I can buy vegetables. I can't buy a painter."

LaVoy answered in kind, "Or a caulker or a rot replacer or a scaffold guy or a....." His voice got higher and trailed off as his hand turned over and over in the open air like a wafting fan.

She answered, "We could just buy a new house, one that's smaller. We could do like Jenny and Bill, just ride in a camper all the time."

LaVoy shot back, "You'd kill me in a week."

She changed the subject. "You hungry?"

He ate the same breakfast, two fried eggs, two pieces of bacon, one cup of grits. He would continue to eat that everyday, work or no work, gardening or painting or loafing. No need in changing things up too much.

CHAPTER 2

The gas can, its red color obscured and stained brown and black from grease and oil and dirt, sloshed back and forth in Jacob's small hands. It knocked against his leg as he shifted it back and forth from his right hand to the left, and sometimes, he would carry the can with both and it would create an awkward sort of gait that his father looked out on and shook his head with an equal mixture of disappointment and humor. Jacob wore sneakers and cut off black shorts and a wrinkled t-shirt and the sweat was beginning to drip from his pale, white legs, his sun burned red face. His dark brown hair stuck up around his ears where it was short and hung around his eyes on top where it was long. Jacob was skinny, average size for his age. He played baseball in March and April, football in August and September. For the rest of the year he carried gas cans, nail guns, wheelbarrows of dirt, and mowed grass with an old lawnmower that stayed broken more than fixed. That was what his father Cap always said.

Jacob's last name was Pellegrin. His father's last name was Pellegrin. His grandfather's last name, too, was Pellegrin. Jacob's father's real name wasn't Cap. It was William. Cap had the lawnmower up on the folded out tailgate of his truck.

Jacob placed the gas can down on the ground, dropping it the final four inches. It made a thud sound as it hit, then faint, high pitches as the liquid popped against the sides of the container before settling. Cap shook his head again. Jacob stood back, then put his hands on his knees and leaned over Cap's shoulder, intently trying to observe what his father was doing.

Jacob's mother, Dani, stepped out onto the porch. The porch was more of a landing, and there was a handicap ramp instead of steps. It had been left there by the people who lived in the house before them. The house was painted a light, mint green. The ramp was also painted green but had been worn down by years of use. Brownish patches of the treated wood showed through the green paint that had been rubbed off. Dani's bare feet scraped against the plywood landing. Suddenly, and with aggravation, she tended to one of them, pulling a splinter out as she spoke.

"Are you fixing that thing again? We need to get the yard mowed before it takes over. It looks terrible."

Cap, annoyed that she was stating the obvious, said, "I know baby; I'll get it soon, I promise."

"Why don't you just go buy another one?"

"I know, I know. Just let me get it this time and we'll talk about it in two weeks."

"In two weeks, it'll be a jungle out here with all this rain we keep getting."

"Yep."

Dani turned, still picking at her foot. Her long pajama bottoms dragged across the rough surface as she opened the generic backdoor. It was one of those with no windows, just metal, paneled bevels meant to imitate the work of a skilled craftsman. All this time, Cap was fiddling with the carburetor. He had finally gotten it off after removing the gas tank and the fuel line. Gas from the half full tank had run out over his hands and down on the ground.

"Damn, I lost the clamp. See if you can find it; it's down

here under the truck I think."

Jacob asked, thinking about what his mother had said, "Why can't you go get another one?"

"You too?" Cap said, turning to look at his son.

Jacob said, "Sorry. Just askin."

"Truth is, I cain't buy another one. Not right now."

Jacob started to search around for the clamp.

"What does it look like?"

"Like a clamp, Son. Goddamnit, here it is." Cap picked up the clamp from underneath his pliers and set it alongside the other one and the fuel line and began spraying the carburetor with cleaner. "Shit, I ain't got time for this."

Jacob asked, "You wanna borrow Mr. Pittman's?" Mr. Pittman was their nearest neighbor. He lived across the field and over a rise on the other side of a strip of oak trees that lined a creek.

"Nope; it'd take more time to do that. Besides, I don't think his is in any better a shape."

"We could try it."

"No, what I need to do is go offshore again. Go do somethin. I'll fix this thing and let you know so you can get started before your Mom loses her mind."

At that, Jacob nodded and walked off toward his friend Vannie's.

CHAPTER 3

Their feet dangled from the bridge, at least they called it a bridge because it connected two pieces of land. All it was were two large timbers cut from a piece of a trestle bridge. Both planks were thick enough so that a tractor could be driven over them, and that was all the bridge was used for, a way for Mr. Pittman to cross over to plow or bush hog or plant his outer fields. That time of year, in the dead of summer close to August, the creosote in the wood became liquid again and gave off its unusually addictive smell. Vannie and Jacob's legs felt it, the sappy black stuff adhering their legs to the wood as they dangled them and kicked out, their white calves widening as they pressed them intermittently to the bridge with each kick. Each had a pile of sticks and rocks, and they were throwing them off the bridge at a beaver dam that seemed to be abandoned.

Jacob asked, "Your dad still offshore?"

"What do you mean?" Vannie asked.

"Is he on his way home?"

"Not til Friday, then he'll be home Saturday, late, or Sunday early."

"My Dad says he's going back offshore."

"Yeah?"

"I guess he's not doing too much around here."

Vannie threw a rock and said, "He's a good welder." To Jacob, this was an ultimate compliment. He always liked it when people said this. It was not the first time he had heard it. He was proud of Cap for doing something that most people couldn't. Cap was known for being good at something, and by the rule of nature, it meant that Jacob had that gift too, regardless of whether or not that was true.

"Seven and seven or month on month off?"

"I don't know. Which is better?"

"Month is what my dad does. Says it gives him more time at home. Less time drivin back and forth to Galveston."

"Where's Galveston?"

"Texas, around Houston."

"And he'll be back Friday?"

"Maybe, if he drives straight through."

Meanwhile, the sticks and rocks continuously pummeled the beaver dam, sending splashes of water onto the dry sticks and small pebbles on the banks of the shallow creek.

"You got a cigar this time?" Vannie asked.

"Nope, couldn't get one."

"You got a magazine?"

"Nope," Jacob said.

"Let's go get somethin ta eat."

"Ok. Just a minute, I'm not finished."

Jacob took the last handful of rocks and dirt and sticks and threw it all at the beaver dam and made a huge commotion, enough to startle a few birds that were perched nearby.

Vannie yelled at Jacob because the dirt had gotten on him. "Shit!"

"Don't be stupid, it ain't wet dirt; don't be such a bitch."

"Fuck you," Vannie said.

They went to opposite sides, unzipped, and peed into the creek, watching the water turn slightly yellow in the ripples as they laughed about it. When Vannie was finished, he shook himself off and slung some on Jacob's leg and ran off. Jacob chased his friend up the small rise and into the open field and hit him playfully across the back of the head as they walked toward Vannie's house to get a snack.

CHAPTER 4

Mora stood in the kitchen. Mora was short for Moriah, where God spoke to David, where Isaac was to be sacrificed. She had on a black pantsuit because she thought it made her look smaller. Her hands were very white and looked solid, like she had worked with them a lot, but with the black painted nails, and the way she always used lotion, they were as beautiful as any woman who had done half the work in half the years. The hands manipulated the butter knife, spreading on peanut butter and jelly, grabbing hot coffee from a filled mug. She sat at the bar, on the chair where she had hung the jacket from her suit, and she brushed back her black curly hair from her white face. She became frustrated with it as if she was concerned about something else. She reached down and grabbed a stray ponytail holder and pulled the hair back quickly and with a sigh, blowing crumbs from the sandwich over the counter. She ate half of her food, not with pleasure or enjoyment but as a function. She slugged down the coffee in the same way. Mora was thankful to herself and her forgetfulness in that she had forgotten her lunch at home and enjoyed this time to herself, even if it was short. She shifted in the seat. Her stomach and breasts rubbed against the tight, form fitting button up shirt as she pulled at it to make it loose. She thought about watching television but realized it was pointless since she had to be back at work in about fifteen minutes. She hated her job, but it was stable, nearly recession proof. In fact, it thrived on recession. The DuPlais Credit and Loan was one of four locations and specialized in short term, medium to high interest loans, for low to moderate income persons. Mora felt bad loaning money to people she knew would have trouble repaying. She knew if they were irresponsible enough to use her business, then they were not responsible enough to pay it back, and that it was downward mobility. But Mora was also a Darwinist, and she looked at it simply as an "us" and "them" struggle for survival.

As she thought about this, a small drop of jelly fell onto the shirt.

"Shit!" She said to the empty house.

She put down what was left of the sandwich and walked to the utility room to get a stain pen. She unbuttoned her shirt and let herself out and breathed deep in the freedom as she rubbed the pen over the stain until it was gone and tossed the shirt in the dryer and leaned back against the dryer with her arms crossed so that her breasts perked up. She looked down and smiled at herself as she jiggled them and thought to herself that some things you never grow out of.

The front door opened, and she could hear footsteps and voices and little noises that came from some undefined place. She knew it was Vannie and Jacob just by those little noises, the way one can recognize a bird call or sitcom theme song.

"You forgot again," Vannie said, giving her a short, one armed hug. Jacob had nodded and already had his head in the pantry.

"Shut up," Mora said playfully.

"Maybe if you took it all at once on Monday, then you wouldn't have too---."

She cut him off by taking the Neptune portion of her

palm, hitting his forehead lightly against it with a sweaty smack. Jacob took out a cereal box and showed it to her, and she nodded that it was ok. Vannie got the milk and, within seconds, they both had their heads buried in the bowls. She sat looking at them intently, like she was looking at two farm animals and told them so. She finished her coffee a little more slowly and wondered to herself if it would be possible. It might be, but she put that thought out of her head and put the mug and plate in the sink. She kissed them both on the top of the head and left.

Jacob spoke first. "Why does she do that? My mom doesn't do that."

"Your mom's a bitch," Vannie said, his mouth dripping with milk and a mouthful of cereal.

They both laughed.

"When's your dad coming home?"

"Damn it man, I told you like three times, this weekend. Listen."

"Dad said he's gonna go offshore."

"You told me that too. Didn't you break a Mercury thermometer in your mouth when we were like five? You need to go get checked out again."

Jacob thought back to his mother, carrying him in her arms rushing into the sliding doors of the emergency room as she was screaming for help. When the nurse had looked him over, she had given him a glass of water and told him to rinse his mouth out at least twenty times and spit into a metal dish shaped like a kidney. She had seen the same thing a million times before.

"You guys get a Fall break this year?" Vannie asked.

Jacob replied, "Maybe."

"They may just give *us* the whole week at Thanksgiving."

"I hope so. We could go camp out at the gravel pit for a day or two."

"You'd go home the first night," Vannie kidded.

"No I wouldn't," Jacob said, suddenly serious about it because his manhood had been challenged, and because he knew it was true.

"Can I stay at your house this weekend?" Vannie asked.

"Probably, I'll ask Dad."

"It's always touchy the first few days my Dad's home. All he wants to do is sit in his chair and drink beer and watch tv. Says he ain't used to bein around that many people either."

"Yeah, come on. You stay over so late anyway, they probably wouldn't notice. Dad might still be fixin that mower." He laughed.

"That why he's goin offshore?" Vannie asked.

"I guess."

"Maybe you could come play with us this year," Vannie said, referring to the junior high football team at his school."

"Dad says your parents are throwing money away so you won't have to be around black people. If you don't have black people, you don't have a football team, if you asked me," Jacob philosophized.

"I don't know, maybe. I just go where they tell me. But at least there ain't nobody pregnant in *my* grade."

"Nobody'd wanna make anybody pregnant at your school. All they got over there is a bunch of ugly snobs and Pentecostals."

"Those Pentecostal ones are the best from what I

hear," Vannie objected.

"Yeah, I heard that too."

They both ruminated on what that meant. Then Vannie broke the silence.

"Let's go back to your house."

The two finished their cereal and left the bowls to warm on the table and went to the woods and the field that separated their two houses.

CHAPTER 5

Jacob's driveway, a mixture of clay and gravel, had a barbed wire fence set against it on one side where Mr. Pittman's cows ate and shit and bred. To the other side there was a small open field that belonged to Cap and Dani where Cap had promised every year to go and plant a stand of pine trees that would pay for Jacob's college. By then, it was too late even to thin them for Jacob. Up at the edge of the field closer to the house sat a horse barn, or what had been a horse barn when Cap still worked in the oilfield. This was the first thing that Jacob and Vannie saw when they came out of the woods and crossed the tar and gravel county road on the way to Jacob's house, the barn set across from them on a little rise, and Cap between them and the barn. They both knew that. The anticipation built as they looked out across the field. Jacob walked over to the brown mailbox he had already checked that morning, pretended to take some time looking in there, then he slammed it back, somewhat in anger about his father still being in the yard tinkering with the lawnmower. They could not see Cap. Often one could not see him, but they knew he was there from the sounds of the footsteps as they walked slowly up the driveway.

Clanging of tools and the slam and high-pitched crunch and creak of the tailgate being closed, these always scared them a little, especially Vannie. Vannie's father had known Cap since they were kids, and Vannie had heard some stories from people about Cap and his temper and how he could fight. Most of it was lies, but it was enough that Vannie remembered and respected it and feared it.

Vannie could also sense something when Cap and his father were around one another, how Vannie's father was referred to as a sort of little brother, that there was a hint of the superior and inferior. It was a struggle that Vannie and Jacob shared likewise, almost as if they were genetically bound to do so, except Vannie was two months older and the situation was reversed.

Cap's truck was a 1980's model Chevrolet with a camper shell on the back. It looked like some massive animal, sounded out with a deep, sputtering, guttural succession of popping as it came down the road. It was already fired up and headed toward them when Jacob and Vannie were halfway up the drive. He saw them and slowed.

His face was darkly tanned, scruffily unshaven, eyes behind aviator sunglasses. The window was always rolled down except in winter when it got too cold to bear. His arm was dark too, hanging elbow out.

"Goin to take this damn mower in to get it fixed, I guess. You boys want anything?"

"Skittles!" Jacob blurted out before he could stop himself. Vannie, like the older brother, looked at him in disappointment.

"Alright." Cap smiled and then looked ahead and started off, spinning gravel as the truck lurched and swayed onto the county road. They waited until he was out of sight and ran as fast as they could to the barn.

It was the middle of summer, and the barn still stunk of horse shit and stale hay. Jacob remembered a year prior, how green the shit was and how fresh the hay had been and how Cap had insisted on keeping the barn as clean as possible and how he called the horses by their names with the same love and care as he would speak to Jacob or Dani, perhaps more so, and how he dressed a certain way with pressed blue jeans and button up shirts tucked in and cowboy boots and a shaved face. Since he had gotten laid off, there was a facet of his father that Jacob had never remembered seeing, that of decline, and worse, defeat. Jacob had begun to spend time with his grandparents when he could in Graceville, Florida, three hundred miles away. He remembered when he had been there for Fall Break how Cap had met them halfway at a restaurant in Mobile and how when Jacob was walking to the car he could see his grandfather patting Cap on the shoulder. Cap was shaking his head in protest as his grandfather was setting some cash on the console. Cap had quickly grabbed it up when Jacob got close enough to give his grandfather a hug goodbye.

And one day, the horses were gone too. It was as simple as that. Jacob had heard them whinnying while he was waiting for the bus out by the mailbox and the stalls were empty that afternoon without a word of explanation from his father. The canned food in the pantry, the ketchup in the fridge, even the fish sticks were all off brands. They wore uniforms at school, but the shoes were really where you could tell who had what and who didn't have much at all. Jacob still had the good shoes, but they were worn thin, and he had devised a plan to wear them as long as possible and save money by gathering scrap metal for Mr. Pittman until he had enough to buy more. He was still fifty dollars shy.

Mr. Pittman always told him, "Never throw away metal cause it'll always pay somethin, just like pulpwood."

The wooden rails where the saddles sat were empty.

The bridles and the striped ropes were all that remained of Prim and Stuckey and BethAnne, Cap's favorite whom he had named after his favorite aunt as a joke.

Jacob and Vannie made their way back through the dank, rotten air and hazy light toward the stalls. Cap had cut the breaker out there months before to save electricity and Jacob was too lazy to walk back up the hill to turn it on. Both ends of the barn were open, with large gates to let the sun in, but the building was long and there were places, especially in the stalls, where there was almost no light except for the odd crack between rough cut oak and pine boards Cap had cut on sight with a portable saw mill. Each of the four stalls had a sliding gate for a door that disappeared behind the wall, the stainless-steel rollers squeaking as they rubbed unoiled against tin tracks. Each door was different, being made by Cap and with no plans. By the time he had gotten to the third one, he had figured it all out. The third door worked better than the others but not near efficiency. Jacob was attempting to open the first door that rocked up and down with each push. Vannie helped and after two minutes of pushing and struggling against the poor design, their own physical weakness, and rust, they had managed a small enough opening for Jacob alone to enter. He kicked at the dirt and shit mixture that he had scooped out a portion of for Dani's use in the flower bed, an excellent compost. He felt his way around as his eyes adjusted. He realized it wasn't as dark as his eyes had made him believe. Each stall also had a place for hay to be dropped from above with four wooden slats large enough for the horse's mouth but small enough to catch the hay and keep it off the ground. In some of these cages, the hay had dried on the outside and remained molded and wet on the inside like a sick kind of candied egg one might eat at Easter. Jacob hated Easter, and he hated hay, and he hated the horses and was glad they were gone because of the work. Each stall also had a shelf that was hung just above Jacob's head, high enough so Jacob could see what was on top if he stood back but not low enough to get at it. He lacked four to six inches being able to reach the shelf and to the back of the shelf. The mower was just high enough so that if he stood on it he could get at the magazines Cap stored up there. Jacob did not have a smartphone or a computer or tablet or anything of the variety. This was all he had. It was all Vannie had as well. In his haste, Jacob wondered why the mower was there, why Cap had lied about taking it, but he put that out of his mind and seized two magazines from the top of the stack. The mower shifted and he fell on the moist ground of the stall.

"Shit!"

"You ok?" Vannie asked with concern.

"Yeah, fell off the goddamn...I fell off the bucket I got up there with."

"Come on before he gets back."

"He ain't comin back for a while I think."

"I wouldn't bet on that," Vannie warned.

Jacob got out of the stall and handed Vannie a magazine to protest.

"I got this one last time, it's nothin but asians."

"Better than nothin."

"Shit," Vannie said, rolling it up and stuffing it behind his back between his underwear and pants.

The two walked out of the barn, their eyes adjusting to the bright summer sun, and split up to go to their own homes.

CHAPTER 6

The sign was what made the strip mall noticeable, but not because of the way it was intended. It had been installed by a company out of New Orleans in 1982 and fluorescent bulbs inside would burn out with intermittence so only part of the lettering showed at one time. It was neither lit or unlit, but stayed in a perpetual limbo like Schrodinger's Cat, dead and alive all at once. The yellow plastic had turned dull and brittle; likewise had the brackets turned where the thing could be taken apart to be cleaned and bulbs changed. The management corporation was located two thousand miles away and paid a little man, Eddie Galloway, a hundred dollars a month to keep it in working order. In turn, Eddie paid his grandson seventy-five and pocketed the rest because he could no longer climb a ladder. Other than changing out the fluorescent tubes every six months, Eddie Galloway III took no more notice of it than he took notice of anything else in his life. He worked out of a Nissan Sentra, circa 1998, and in the trunk he kept the tools he needed for his diversified occupations, pool chemicals, drywall mud floaters and trowels, a miter saw, and various cleaning supplies, a broom, lemon pledge. His grandfather had kept a nice, neat truck, a 1970 Chevy Luv, still pristine, not even a piece of small trash allowed in the truck bed. The dash was greased and slick and dustless. The engine ran the same as it did when he bought it from the dealership. Eddie III's car sounded like the Battle of the Somme as it rattled down the road.

With a quick look at these two, Eddie I and Eddie III,

one could see the degradation that had occurred in that town in just two generations, proof beyond doubt that the idea of "idle hands" is indeed a certainty. Where Eddie I had the Korean War and a steady job, a wife dead after fifty years of marriage, and a pension when he retired, Eddie III had the War on Terror, whatever that meant, and small, frittering occupations that lasted only as long as it took him to quasi finish the work and then blow the cash in hand at whatever roadside bar he chose and to support with inconsistency the three kids he had with two different women. And aside from all of this, he had discovered something new, something different than alcohol that made him work faster, talk wiser, and feel like he had touched Jesus' hem. This was becoming his fourth child.

The strip mall sign had been put up during the peak of that community, bright yellow with all bulbs blazing new, a grocery store, insurance agency, real estate firm, and a tire place on the end. It represented more than business. It represented what had been an American experiment with the most promising data, a working but prosperous lower class, a professional, wealthy group of lawyers and businessmen and doctors, and a still larger middle class made up of small business owners, teachers, law enforcement officers, and factory supervisors.

By the time Cap drove into the strip mall that morning, the tire place was selling out its stock so Mr. Pickens could retire with his newest wife in the Florida Panhandle. The grocery store was barely functioning, and every business looked either abandoned or was a temporary check cashing outfit preying on the growing class of unemployed, unskilled laborers. The exception was the vape shop where Cap was going to visit his sister, named after their grandmother, Sera.

It was hot; there was no shade to fight it.

The vape shop was new, and it stood out with its modern architectural facade, like a piece of Sweden in Mississippi, crisp and new, sharp angles and straight edges, beautiful flat toned woods and earthy colors of green and light blue mixed with industrial looking metals, stainless, spotless. Even the name was classy. Whereas many of these places had names like VapeNation, Vapecloud, and High Volume Vapors, Sera's place with its sleek look and feel, had a sign with industrial iron stamping, Vaporous Oils and Notions Inc.

Sera was behind the counter, surrounded by an army of pipes, boxes of various scented nicotine cartridges, and a gathering of multiple user hookahs. The place smelled of vanilla, which Cap always enjoyed, along with the cool air that hit him as soon as he would enter the place. Sera was several years younger than him. She had been born when he was a freshman in high school, and he still remembered carrying her around in his sweaty football uniform after a game as the fellow players and cheerleaders fawned over the little red headed, pink faced baby who seemed as happy as ever to be soaked in sweat on a cold October night. He had been a sort of third parent for her. Their parents had been older and took little care, or were very naive in their care for her, so Cap stood in. He checked out boyfriends and followed up on her stories of staying the night at one place and attempting to go elsewhere. He had looked out for her and given her the care that any parent would give their own child, but in the years since, their parents had moved to Graceville. Sera had become a self-assured woman, complete with an associate's degree.

Their roles had begun, slowly, to reverse themselves. Where she had gone to see Cap about her problems, he had started coming to see her, and they would sit in the shop and talk and drink coffee in the corner while Sera waited on the odd customer, her wild, beautiful red hair, stroked gently by her hand as she turned down to concentrate on pouring custom mixes for a select clientele, mostly local drug dealers or New Orleans folk that only enjoyed Mississippi on the weekends or for quick mid-week romps on the river. The hair would then bounce right back. She never wore anything to restrict it.

Her personality was the opposite of his. Where he was withdrawn, sort of mysterious, some might mistake for crazy, she was outgoing and snarky and sexy, which gave her a different sort of power over people. They both possessed this quality. And because she was outgoing, she had acquired friendships, partnerships, connections to people of all classes in that town and surrounding communities. She attended both the large Baptist church in town and the weekly river parties on one of the multitude of camps that sat on the riverbanks between there and the Louisiana state line. She could call on them for help, help getting permits for local contractors, help getting the strip mall parking lot cleaned off by the city, and in getting jobs for people, mainly her brother. These conversations were always the same, taking place at the end of their visits, and that was what made it strange, that Cap would ask so quickly.

"Slow down Hoss. What's the matter?" she said as she wiped a counter down with glass cleaner.

"I gotta go back offshore."

"Don't do that; you won't be home. Jacob'll turn bad."

"Won't matter if he don't have a house to live in."

"There ain't much out there right now, you know that."

"Might have to go month on month off, overseas."

"Even then..." She said, walking over to the coffee pot for a refill.

"This is awful," Cap said, pushing the bitter grounds from between his bottom lip and teeth.

"It's the last from that container; it's always bad."

"Well open anuthern."

"Just drink it, jackass."

Annoyed, he put down his mug. She walked over and filled the cup again.

"I don't want no more."

"Let me make a call in a minute. Sherry over at Smith's might have somethin at least for today. I sent a kid over there last week and he ain't been back to bother me. They must've kept him. I guess I'm the only game in town since the WIN Mississippi shut down."

"Helluva lot more effective," Cap added.

"Aahh," she said lovingly.

She tossed back her hair and swiped her phone open and sent a text to Sherry.

"Wait here a minute. She said she'd get right back."

CHAPTER 7

Dani heard the fast succession of footsteps, so she knew it couldn't be Cap. Nevertheless, she turned the speakerphone off, and the voice that would have been fully audible anywhere in the house was muted so that only high pitched chirps could be heard as Dani picked up the phone from the warm clothes. She held it to her ear with her shoulder and balanced it while holding the clothes basket.

Jacob nodded to her as he went by, turning slightly so she wouldn't see the bulge where the magazine was visibly stuffed between his lower back and shorts. Dani nodded too, quickly over her shoulder as she went into the living room and set the basket down on the couch. She heard the door to his room shut with a short, sharp creak and brush from the carpet.

"Yeah, yeah *I know*," Dani said.

Muffled tone.

"*Well*, he wouldn't be, that's the thing."

Muffled tone.

"Just give me a second." She pushed the basket to the other side of the couch.

Muffled tone.

"I don't know where he went. Lawnmower I think."

Muffled tone.

"Yeah. I will."

Muffled tone.

"I cain't right now."

Muffled tone.

Then Dani chided the voice in a parental tone. "How

old are you? *Really*? This is ridiculous."

Muffled tone.

Dani spoke quickly then with a whispering, almost completely muted, tone as she looked toward Jacob's room.

"Miss you too."

She tapped the screen and set the phone on the couch and began folding the clothes until the basketful was stacked and ready.

When Jacob was finished, he flipped the magazine over so that it lay face down. Staring back at him then were only ads and promises for the next issue, girls of the Southwestern Conference, a spread with Miss September from two years before. Jacob was unsure exactly where it came from, that small amount of remorse he felt as he cleaned himself off with an old t-shirt he kept stuffed under the bed. He didn't understand brain chemistry, releases of serotonin and dopamine, and so he processed it through one of the few prisms he did understand, religious guilt. Nor did he understand why he felt such a compulsion to do it. He, like an animal, just *did* without thinking.

The floor of Jacob's room was covered with old food containers, chip bags, etc. There was within this mass a snaking of video game wiring cables that led like veins and arteries to the console heart and a twenty-inch flat screen television seated on a four-legged lunch tray. He would sit for hours and play, huddled in a rickety office chair he had found in Mr. Pittman's driveway. Next to the television, a tall five drawer dresser, held up by a brick on the front right corner, loomed over him as he played, looking down on him and casting an inflated shadow when the afternoon sun beamed in from a small sliding glass window. The window was high enough that he never had to pull the blinds down to hide anything he did in his room. It gave him confidence and added some mystery to his space, like watching someone through a keyhole or over the top of a parapet. He felt safe knowing that he could see them if he wanted to, but not the other way around. Trophies on top of the dresser would make miniature baseball and soccer silhouetted figurines on the wall above him. But, as he lay in the bed that day, there were no shadows yet. It was just after lunch and the sun had not yet crossed over in its descent. In fact, the sun had not been out much all day even though it was extremely hot and muggy. "Gumbo weather," his grandmother had called it.

He wasn't sure what to do. He was tired, a little hungry, and most of all, bored.

In the mind of people, no matter how seemingly trivial or ridiculous, there is always a familial thing that makes a person feel secure. Sometimes it is impossible to notice, or it seems that people just forget and take it for granted. In Jacob's room, always hanging on the wall, was a welder's cap, a tiny brimmed thing made to be worn backwards. The design of such caps might remind one of the outrageous and flashy garb of a golfer: sharp, bright colors, insane designs, and on and on. Some men wore pink ones in October.

In the mornings, before school, he would look at it as he lay in bed, much like he was that summer afternoon, thinking of his father, but more so thinking of his father's way of life and how he hoped not to repeat it. Then, without noticing, he stopped. The cap became like the trophies, forgotten things on a day to day basis. But, in his subconscious it remained, however, like the sound of his mother's voice, or the number of steps it took to go from the kitchen to the front door, the way he would avoid being struck by the barn door when he opened it by dodging quickly to his right.

It was like a guitar player, movements of memory by muscle and feel, incognizant things, his vision the keys and frets on the board.

It was covered with an eight-ball design, and some rust, and some char mixed with the rust, caked with sweat salt. Jacob would not have noticed the thing, never minded it for a minute, except on that day, when he saw that it was gone. He turned his body up and around in the bed and jumped off onto a layer of dirty clothes and walked over to the dresser and found the cap. He brushed it off and returned it to the nail. Then he went back to the bed and placed his hands behind his head and stared at the cap and at the wall and at the light beginning to hit the wall from the tiny secluded window of his own little flophouse.

Dani always began softly and motherly, then increased to a bear.

"Jacob. Jacaaaahb!"

"Yeah?" Jacob answered through the locked door.

"I'm going out for a minute to the store."

"Ok. Can you bring me some skittles?"

"Damn it, Jacob, no. I'll be back in a minute."

"Alright, chips then."

"Maybe; I'll see."

Jacob knew what that meant, that she was lying about getting them, like his father lied about the lawnmower, like Jacob had lied about never looking at those magazines or ever using them.

It made him feel a little better to know he would never outgrow it.

CHAPTER 8

Sera still attempted to convince Cap to stay close to home for work. "You could get somethin, maybe pipe fitting at the shipyard. An hour commute."

"Yeah, I guess. Too much drivin though."

"As opposed to two days on a plane?"

"I can handle it all at once."

Smiling and shaking her head. "You don't make any sense. You know it'd be better to work about an hour or so away, but you didn't think about that. You already had your mind made up and that's that. Just admit it, you're wrong."

She spoke to him while picking up her phone that had begun to buzz and ding.

"Says she has something; crew's down a man."

"Weldin?"

"Roustin."

"Shit." He shook his head and picked up his coffee for the first time in a while, running his hand in his pocket across the tiny brimmed eight ball cap. "They still doin it the same way?"

"Cash money?"

"Yeah."

"I reckon so."

"Tell her I'll be there in a minute."

"She says they already left but she called em. They're stopping for lunch at the Drive-Up." Drive-Up was a fast-food restaurant with stalls for ordering and no drive through.

"I'll meet them."

"Ok," Sera said. He hurriedly set the mug on the countertop and offered her a quick look of thanks before leaving. As the chime sounded and her brother disappeared in the parking lot, she heard Shelton's truck with its glass packs pulling up in back. The back door opened and closed with a slam. The fresh, humid air burst from underneath the door that opened to the back office and storeroom. Sera loved that smell.

CHAPTER 9

Jacob emerged from his room and slid down the hall, the magazine recklessly fixed in his hand. As he walked across the sparse lawn that had become overgrown, he kicked at the forks of bahia grass. He opened the gate that led to the barn and the rusty roundpen. He didn't lock it or even loop the chain. There were no animals left to escape the enclosure. Grass had crept into the area that had been only dirt surrounding the barn. Hoof prints were turning green and fuzzy, cracking as he stepped on them. It was like popping plastic bubble wrap; each time he walked out there he would crunch a few more. It was his way of erasing the memory of ever having those horses. He could still see Cap out there in the round pen, BethAnn on one end of a tether, Cap guiding her around in circles. Jacob had always been amazed at how his father never got dizzy. And then there was the shoveling, and the constant fixing of broken tools, pens, trucks, lawnmowers, and then credit. Then, as on that day, silence, silence except underneath his feet as the green cornflakes of horse hooves cracking beneath his small weight and the brittleness brought on by the southern drought. Storm. Nothing. Storm. Nothing. Feast and famine, just like the oil field.

Cap's truck was unmistakable as it slowed to make the right turn, but by then, Jacob was inside the barn, the magazine was on the shelf, and the boy peered out through a crack in the wall to see his father jump out of the truck which he left running and emerge seconds later in a blue work suit and boots and a hard hat under his arm.

There was a pack of skittles on the table in the kitchen.

CHAPTER 10

Shelton Brooks stood six feet, with dull red hair and a girthy, well-worn, used up body. He had worked in the oil field since dropping out of school at seventeen years old. He worked as a Roustabout, Roughneck, then Pusher and Driller on several offshore rigs before moving to land where he managed a series of wells for the company he would later buy out when it went into bankruptcy in the 1980's. Never a great or motivated student, he had become the antithesis of both in the real world of business. To buy the company, he put up everything he owned, his house, a large plot of family land, and convinced his first wife's father to invest. Later on, Shelton would force his father in law into an early retirement, setting him up to look more incompetent than he already was, putting a magnifying glass to it, turning the workers and his own daughter against him until the old man was forced to go home, in roughly the same financial shape he was in before, house and land rich, cash poor. After his first divorce, Shelton offered to pick up the note on the old man's vintage car collection. Instead of paying the notes, he let them go until default. The bank took the cars. Shelton then went in and bought up the house and the land for cheap. Then Shelton married a car hop from the Drive-Up, a girl named Rinzi, and set down to have a whole litter.

They only had Robert.

Since then, Shelton grew the company, screwed anyone he wanted, including two preacher's wives and a series of office workers he referred to as "Ass-sistants." Rinzi went through stages of looking the other way and caring enough to have him followed, but never asked for a divorce, most likely because Shelton was well enough connected at that point to debunk any story, even one with picture and audio evidence.

Shelton owned the vape shop where Sera worked. Sera never gave him all the power, and he fed on it like a drug because he could never conquer her. In giving him the sense that he *would* conquer her, she held somewhat of a power over him. She had made a habit of it with most people; Shelton was just another thing, a method or means of survival in that small, declining town where Eddie I was giving way to Eddie III, and then Eddies IV and V.

"You need to keep this thing locked," Shelton said, pushing the door to the office open with a meaty hand.

"Why would I do that Shelton? I'm right here."

"Never know who might come in here."

"I know," she said, smiling and gesturing toward him with her hand.

"Had many in today?"

"About the same," Sera replied.

"Allen been here?"

"I haven't seen him in a week."

Shelton became suddenly annoyed. "Shit."

He began shuffling through the desk, opening and slamming doors.

"You can ask me where somethin is without tearin up my goddamn desk."

"Cheaters. Mah readin glasses."

"They ain't here."

"Well, where are they?"

"Trash. I broken em the other day by accident. Threw em out," she said with a sense of joy.

"Fuck," he said sharply, then squinted at the computer screen and clutched the mouse and made it disappear so that it looked like only his hand was guiding the thing like a magician.

She walked back to the front of the store when she heard the doorbell chime.

"Logged me out of ma email too!" he said loudly so she could hear.

"Yep!" The storeroom door closed halfway through her saying it.

"Goddamnit," Shelton said, still squinting, typing his information, "BigSquall@nettyhoo.com." After typing, backspacing, typing, cursing, he finally maneuvered and got back in and began reading through the emails from Colorado, his lawyer, ads for Filipino women because he had clicked on something two years prior.

When the bell chimed again she came back, and he grabbed her around the waist and pulled her next to him and smelled her jeans and tight t shirt and pressed his face to her stomach and made a disgusting sound of pleasure derived from it. She reached back and closed the door and began to give him the illusion that he owned her and knew her unlike the rest of them, exacted her power over him. Her body was of little consequence, and so, if it helped her, she would gladly spend it like a currency in small, precise increments to get what she wanted.

CHAPTER 11

The river made sloshing sounds and gathered foam against the stubborn branches and pieces of branches that clung to the banks and sunken logs. Up above the river, up the sharp, steep banks, sat an observation area for picnics made of sun baked treated wood. Three beams acting as arms held the octagonal structure out over the bluff and kids made a habit of gathering rocks from the gravel parking lot and tossing them into the swirling river, romantic, subtle, with hidden undercurrents and a covert swiftness. It bespoke the Old Woman of Hansel and Gretel lore, the peaceful and parental, the Old Man, the father, cloaked in a father's love with an underlay, seething of violence and danger.

It was so hot on the deck that Dani felt heat moving slowly through the thin soles of her shoes, scorching her feet so that she rotated, putting one on top of the other to slow it still further. Through a thick, green hardwood stand of oaks and sweetgum and sycamore, she could see her car. She glanced at it every few moments, waiting anxiously, constantly vigilant. There were no other cars in the parking lot. A single massive oak branch gave her body shade while her feet and most of her bare legs cooked, offering some relief to the midday heat. It was too hot even for the squirrels who usually ran about over the splintery railing. All Dani could hear of these things was leaves being tossed and crumpled in the woods, squirrels like dolphins in open water, bobbing up and down out over the dried top layer and tiny birds tap dancing across the leaves, pecking for small worms and insects. She looked back and saw one, slow then fast, up then down. When she turned to look there was one more car in the lot, an SUV pulled next to her small compact.

CHAPTER 12

"Who was that who come in?" Shelton asked Sera. She finished pulling up her pants and slid her shoes on and checked the front of her shirt. She knew she should have taken it off, but it was fine.

"Who, that? Greg Copton, you know him. Why?"

"I mean before, when I first got here," Shelton asked, knowing the answer.

CHAPTER 13

The pavilion opened at the top into four squares that faced out vertically toward the river, wind catchers designed to send gusts down into the open space below.

"We used to have birthday parties there when I was a kid," Dani said as she kicked her feet across the splintery wood and looked out to their cars, feeling a short, welcomed breeze.

Mora, still in her pants suit from work, had taken off the jacket and left it in the car. She sat with her feet up on the bench, her hands clasped just under the knees so that the veins jumped out a little.

"You're sweating," Dani said.

"It's hot." She yawned. "I wish this wind would keep going."

"I know." Dani reached over and wiped the sweat from Mora's forehead with her hand.

"Your hands smell like softener."

"I was doing laundry when you called."

"He's off fixing the lawnmower?"

"Yeah, today..."

"Tomorrow?"

"It'll be somethin else," Dani answered in a defeated tone. "You know he'll stay busy."

"You need more money?"

"No, I'll be alright. You don't have to keep doing that. I feel bad. I can't pay you back."

"I told you not to worry about that."

Dani sighed and blew a raspberry between her lips.

"What are you thinking?" Mora asked.

"I hated birthday parties then, and I sure hate em now."

"When was the last time you took Jacob to a birthday party?" Mora laughed sarcastically, brushing her hair back from her face. Dani began to laugh too.

"Shut up," Dani said. "When I was a kid, the only thing I liked was throwing rocks through those openings. I never could get that high up, but Sean could do it every time. Mama told him not to throw rocks in the pavilion, so we got in the pavilion and threw em out. He hit her car and busted out the windshield." She referred to her brother.

"Sounds like him. I mean, it sounds like what you said he was like, like he was...You get what I'm saying," Mora said, giving up.

"I gotta get another job."

"School starts back before you know it. You can't get by til then?"

"Doesn't matter anyway. I'll be broke anyhow," Dani said.

"You two dollar yourself to death."

"Damn it, I'm serious. I gotta get somethin else. Go back to nursin school or something."

"You couldn't give people shots."

"I bet I could if I had to, and it's gettin to that point." Her voice slowly trailed off and she looked down.

"Hey. Hey!" Mora said, slapping Dani's thigh.

"What?" Dani said.

"You know it doesn't have to be like all that."

Dani spoke again, but this time in a staccato voice, emphasizing each syllable. "I just don't understand where it goes."

"What?"

"Time."

"That's what I'm saying. Hey, look up. That's what I'm saying." Mora reached over again and touched her knee, then clutched it, feeling Dani's bare kneecap.

"It's not that easy," Dani said.

"You think *this* is?"

"Let's just sit here."

"Couple of old lezbos."

"I ain't no dyke," Dani said.

"You know what I mean," Mora relented.

"I don't like it when you say things like that."

Mora hit her in the knee. "I know. Sorry, Bitch."

They both laughed and looked off.

"It would be better than travel ball," Mora said.

"End up with havin ta talk ta Pam about freezing bats and teaching her piece a shit boy to throw a knuckle ball. No thanks, not worth it."

"Need to get back?"

"Yeah," Dani said. "Finish laundry."

"I think I am gonna take Vannie to get a hamburger later. I'll take Jake too."

"Alright, sounds good," Dani said, getting up and stretching.

"Miss you," Mora said, walking away.

"You too," Dani returned as they began to walk down the wooden ramp, close side by side.

Even Dani had gotten used to the way it was; the idea that things could be misconstrued bothered her less and less. This never seemed to bother Mora. Mora was more daring and cavalier, but her feelings were hurt that much easier. Mora was a new razor sharp needle that punctured the fabric quickly then fell back beneath while Dani was a little used and blunt; it took more force to feed the thread, but she would keep punching through each time, slowly wearing down until nothing was left.

Mora would break.

THE AFTERNOON OF

CHAPTER 1

At first, Jacob pulled at the cord. He pulled so much that he was out of breath. The skittle candy taste, the citrus and strawberry vapors plumed from his closed mouth and up through his nostrils. He kept pulling until his arm went to sleep. Then he sat back and rested himself on a five-gallon bucket. The melding of excrement and rotten and fermented grass blew from one end of the barn to the other. As he rested, the wind was blowing from the opposite end to cool him off, but with it, the wind brought the smells. He took the candy out and forced a handful into his mouth. He twisted the red bag and trapped the remaining pieces and forced it down into his sweaty pocket. He wiped his face with his hand and caught his breath and kicked at the dark brown dirt and looked out at the sun that was creeping closer and closer to him.

Clug, clug, clug, it had sounded, almost turning over. Jacob even thought he'd heard it catch one time and begin to turn the blade, but it was just wishful thinking, his imagination, an hallucination that he could do something his father could not. Possibly Cap had missed the obvious thing that was causing the mower to malfunction. Jacob had a dream that Cap would come home and the yard would be mostly cut, or completely cut and he would wonder how, why, then he would see Jacob and Jacob would feel good about that, but not so good it showed. Jacob would be cool and unsurprised by it, calmly humble and self-effacing.

"*I just added gas and pulled it,*" he would say. "*Maybe you just flooded it.*" Perhaps he would tell his father that.

Cap would be angry about it a little, then he would scruff up Jacob's hair and put him in a headlock and tell him where he'd gone in his work clothes, why he'd lied about going to get the mower fixed. Then Cap would *have* to tell him. There was no denying it had been left in the barn.

Jacob took out the rest of the candy and untwisted the bag and ate the rest while he stared again at the dead machine. Still chewing, he walked over to the red six drawer tool box and opened it and looked for the socket set and found the pieces and put them in his pocket. He knelt down by the mower and began to fit them onto the outer housing until he found the right one. He began to take the bolts off one by one, each time looking for an irregularity, not that he knew what an irregularity would look like. At first, he tried to keep everything in little piles with the pieces and parts and bolts laying together so he could reconstruct it all later. The deeper he went, the worse and more strewn the piles became, until finally, he had gone so far he couldn't remember how anything fit back together, not the parts or the bolts or anything. It all sat before him in a mound of greasy metal and hard plastic and caked grass coated in a layer of oil and gasoline. His hands were black all over. Even his fingernails were driven into by the dark dirt and dead skin where he'd clawed his arms in response to the indignant summer heat. As long as he had worked at removing bolts and taking off housing and undoing the gas tanks and flywheel, Jacob's brain had been occupied and driven toward some sort of goal. He worked as hard as he could ever remember, and he sweated more and he cursed more. But in the end, there was a pile of useless pieces, and he had no idea where any

of them went, and he began to panic,
    wiping sweat from his forehead,
    leaving finger streaks,
    heat bumps,
    heat rash,
    black marks heat rash streaks.
    "What was a clamp?"
    "It looks like a clamp Son," Cap had said.

Vannie walked up.

"Shit!" He bent over and began to laugh. Then he saw Jacob's face. He had seen that look before. He had made it himself.

"What'd you do man?"

"Tryin ta fix it. We cain't afford another one."

"Your dad already back with it?"

Jacob hesitated. "Yep...he uhhh.. he went back to town for somethin, maybe to get another one but I don't know."

"Needs one. Grass is gettin high," Vannie observed.

"Can I borrow yours?"

"*I'm* not pullin that all the way over here!"

"I know. I'll get it," Jacob said.

"I need to ask my mom. She's out though. Town must be jumpin. Dad bring those skittles?"

"Nope," Jacob lied again.

Vannie looked out at the yard again, making a show of sticking his head around the opening. "It ain't that bad. If he gets one by the end of the week, it'll be fine. I can get ours by then. We'll just do it during the day. I won't have to ask. But shit, then Dad'll be here. I don't know," he said, thinking aloud.

"Don't worry about it."

"You still plannin on fixin it?"

"Whadda you think?" Jacob said, throwing the carburetor down next to the pile.

"I think you're gone be in a shit ton a trouble when Cap gets home," Vannie said, laughing again. "I'm just glad it ain't me!"

"He's gonna be pissed."

"If you think he got another one, he'll just forget about it. Just put it somewhere else."

"What?"

"Just put it up somewhere. I bet he won't notice it's even gone."

"I think I might just throw it out altogether then. He might think someone stole it."

"Don't know why anyone would steal this. You know it ain't worth much even as scrap. An you cain't scrap it without Cap findin out so it don't matter."

"I know," Jacob said. "Help me put this shit in the wheelbarrow."

Jacob was back from the house in a few minutes, rolling the wheelbarrow so as not to break the rusted frame. Vannie had spent the time kicking at the pile of metal, scattering it a little and thinking.

"Need to bury it if we put it in the woods. Cap would find it probly."

"You probly right. I think I might roll it down and throw some of it in the culvert and then some out on Mr. Pittman's land."

"It's your ass anyway. I don't really care. I'd just throw it all out by the road somewhere and don't say nothin about it unless somebody finds it. But that's just me," Vannie said.

"I need to spread it out."

"It ain't rye grass seed! This grass is so thick anyway. But whatever it better be quick. You need some help?"

"I'll put it behind the house by the air conditioner. Take it out tonight or tomorrow after they leave."

"I'm gone go home then. Need a tarp?"

"Nope. They never go back there," Jacob said.

"Alright."

"You bring it back?" Jacob said, referring to the magazine.

"Not finished with it yet. I'll bring it back tomorrow."

"Finished a bunch already I bet." Jacob punched him in the arm.

"You got room to talk?"

"Maybe *your* dad'll bring some back this time," Jacob said hopefully.

"Maybe, I'll let you know," Vannie said as he turned to walk away.

"What'd you come over for anyway?"

"Heard you cursin from over where I was walkin on Pittman's."

"That far? Shit."

"He'll probably call this evenin and talk to Dani." Vannie laughed, pointing to Mr. Pittman's field.

"Shit. I bet he does. Fuck it."

Vannie walked off as Jacob put the parts into the wheelbarrow. He looked up each time after he knelt down to put things in and noticed that Vannie got a little farther away each time until he was gone altogether. The last thing he did was fold up the handle and put it on top and tried to make it stay. After several attempts, he took the handle and threw it in another stall and covered it with hay. He could get that later.

He turned the wheelbarrow toward the house and began to make his way up the path to the house. Even though it was beaten down, there were several rough spots and divots in the grass path. He had to stop twice to put parts back in when the thing shifted and he lost control. When he got to the driveway, he was near running with it. The rattling wheelbarrow was so loud it muted out Dani's car. Jacob had been looking down when he raced up the driveway to the carport they used only half of. He ramped up the small bump going in and rounded the corner and parked it all behind the rusty outdoor air unit. It was then that he heard the car door open and looked around the corner of the house to see dust settling in the driveway.

He and his mother locked eyes in the shade of the carport. The damp coldness of the sweaty concrete floor gave off a smell of gas and oil and mixed to near perfection with the look on her face. That here, there was one more thing to have to do. That "*What is it gonna take?*" look.

"Do I have to stay here all damn day to watch you?" She asked, motioning him inside, up the ramp to the kitchen.

CHAPTER 2

Sera knew she had to answer. She didn't feel like lying to him. She *could* lie to him though, easily. And Shelton would believe her. But, as always, she knew her window of time was small and short. Shelton would promise anything before or after they had visited her office. This was the thing that made him human. It made him vulnerable. She felt good about that. She felt good that she was the only one. She felt good knowing it could stay that way so long as she scooped it out and fed it to him in small amounts over a lengthy period of time, fractured fulfillments of her own empty and small, meaningless promises. The delay, the anticipation, turned him back into a little boy, his mother offering him no more than cake batter on a beater, ten minutes of television before bed. Sera took him back there, led him, nurtured him, and made him forget about death and responsibility for only a little while. She tempted him with her mysteries and illusions. Again, her body cost her nothing, and it meant nothing to her. *One man's junk is another man's treasure.* She would think to herself. Then she could ask for anything.

"Cap," she said.

"Oh, I thought it was."

"Why'd you ask then?"

"Always like to hear you say it. I know he's your family but it ain't like he's gotta come over here all the time."

"He doesn't come over here all the time," she said, touching Shelton's unshaven face, thumb on his lower lip and finger under his rough chin. He pulled away from her.

"No, just when he needs somethin. What was it this time? You give him some money?" He was sitting back in the office chair. He leaned back and began buckling his pants, trying not to show her how much he was sucking in to button them.

"I've never given him any money."

"Bullshit."

"He wouldn't take it no way."

"I wouldn't put anything past that sumbitch. What are you doing next weekend?"

She was somewhat annoyed at his changing the subject. She was in the mood for a good fight. "Nothin I don't guess."

"Rinzi's goin to the Dixie Market in Jackson to pick up some shit. Stayin there with her mother. Wanna go to the coast?"

"I don't understand why you can't just hire him back full time."

"Honey, no matter what goes on betweenxt me an you, that fucker ain't never workin at Smith's *ever* again." He said the name of his company like a mother reprimanding a child. "You wanna go to the coast er not? Or you can just stay over instead if you want."

"I ain't stayin at your place. Smells like fluffy dogs and plug in air freshner."

"I'll unplug it all and put the dog at the vet."

"I guess I could eat some seafood," she said, thinking of the salty iodic fried shrimp she always liked to get down there. "I'll letcha know. I ain't done talkin about the other though."

"Well I am. I'm damn sick a talkin about it." He got up from the chair.

"You workin off today?"

"No, I gotta stay in the office. Gotta guy comin in about those tapped out wells in Raleigh. We're about done gettin em ready."

"Yeah?"

"If that pans out it'll keep me floatin right on inta retirement."

"What would you do with free time?"

"Anything I want. Buy a boat and fish when I want to."

"You can't fish."

"I'd have plenty of time ta learn then. Drink as much beer as I need to."

"What about the other thing with Allen? Is that just icin on the cake?" she asked.

"That'll be enough to buy Rinzi's ass out and keep her in little dogs and antiques an plug in freshners her whole life." He laughed and tried to slap Sera's butt, but she turned and he missed her. "Man!" He chased her into the front of the store, then stopped and went into a coughing spell.

"Damn!" Sera said laughing at him. "Too much in one day?"

"Maybe. Maybe not," he said, leaning on the counter to recover.

"You just gonna leave Boy Robert in charge?"

"Ha! That's a good one."

"Well I'm busy tonight with church," Sera said.

"What about church?"

"Me and the old women are making dinner for the high school band camp kids."

"You and bunch of old bitches and chicken pie. What time do I need to be there?"

"Speakin of the other..." she spoke abruptly. "Have you talked ta Allen?"

"I haven't talked to him in about three days. I'm gone go by his grandma's if I can't get him to answer his phone by tomorrow. He's got shit to do. I gotta meet that guy in a little while about them tapped out wells. He said they might be back online in a month if it works. I'll see ya later maybe."

"Maybe not," she said. "And it ain't chicken pie, it's chicken spaghetti."

"Bring some home. I'll stop by."

"I'll be too late."

"I bet if those wells work out and I get hold of Allen it won't be too late," he said, half sticking out the door by then.

"We'll see. Nobody's fool enough to marry you but Rinzi Deevers. Cause she's as used up as them wells."

"I ain't said nothin about marryin. I ain't gone be a deacon no way."

"You're lettin all the air out," Sera chided.

"Yep, an I'll pay for it. Sell some shit today." He laughed and let the door chime closed then turned around and slung it open again and walked back by her through the store, realizing his truck was in back. She smiled at him with a hint of evil and joy.

"You let me do that! I got shit to do," he said, hitting the glass counter and storming out the back. His glossy oxford blue truck lifted high in the air with all the latest paraphernalia of winches and hitches and a mountain of other trinkets that shined with unused chrome brilliance. He hit the gas and chugged at her as he sped around the end of the strip mall and bounded across the near empty parking lot. The only people out that time of day were retired Baptist widows shopping at the last small grocery store in town. “H.A. Smith Oilfield Services” sparkled grey from the driver’s side door.

She turned away but could hear him hitting the speed bumps and revving the motor.

CHAPTER 3

Shelton's son Robert sat in the parking spot of the Drive-Up. The work truck was at one time the same color as his father's, but it was covered with dust and dirt, mud caked around the tires, clay cooked to a ceramic consistency around the tailpipe. Shelton liked it that way. It made them look busy. They were.

Robert was twenty-two, fresh from college where he had dropped out. It was a benevolent gesture made by the Dean, allowing him to withdraw before he was expelled. All that was fixed to his school record by then was a withdrawal failing label so that no one in the future could tell whether he'd had to leave school to nurse a sick family member or in truth had hazed a freshman from Iuka to the point the young man ended up in the hospital for three weeks with alcohol poisoning. An apology, an excuse of youthful ineptness, was not enough to suffice in the eyes of the Dean. The papers and local news had picked it up.

Robert was asked to leave.

Robert was an example.

His dark brown hair was scruffy and long down over his ears and curled up around his ears and faded red St. Louis Cardinals baseball cap. Ozzie Smith and Stan Musiel were unknown to him. Mark McGuire, Kent Mercker, and Brian Jordan took prominent places.

Robert, unbeknownst to the crew joining him in the truck, was working for half wages to pay off what his father had in tuition those three and a half years though he was nowhere near a degree. Robert had only been staying around college for its lack of responsibility and the surplus of clueless coeds who flooded in every year from Bay St. Louis, Jackson, Old and New South sluts from Natchez and Greenville, people who would talk about heritage and Southern things but couldn't name where Stonewall Jackson had died of friendly fire or knew that Arlington Cemetery had been Lee's home before the war.

That Jeff Davis was a cyclops, and on and on.

Robert slid his card in the slot and waited for approval, and five minutes later the girl appeared with their food: hamburger and fry combos for he and Allen, a chocolate malt for Mr. John, the master welder. Hot or cold, big job or small job, Mr. John always ate ice cream for lunch. When they didn't stop at a drive thru, he was content to buy a pint from a gas station. He didn't care if it was frozen over, expired, or what flavor it was. When they asked him why he did this, he at first told them it was none of their damned business and set to grinding a metal spoon he carried with him each day down into a solid chunk of frozen vanilla, butter pecan, or dutch chocolate swirl. Robert, as a boy, remembered this about Mr. John and respected his being different. He remembered asking about it as a kid and Shelton had told him that when you do something for long enough sometimes you forget why you do it, then told the boy to rake sycamore leaves off the front lawn of H.A. Smiths' office and mind *his own* damned business.

There was mystery to it, and Robert would bring it up sometimes. Mr. John would tell him to mind his business again and again Robert and the other ones, a revolving door of roustabouts, would examine the mystery that would go unsolved. Then maybe there wasn't a mystery. Maybe Mr. John was just different. There may have been no more than that. And the conversation would continue. Maybe Robert and John and whatever roustabout, whatever helping gopher, would keep it going. People like mysteries and discovery. It is the only true mode of education. Being able to keep a mystery and hold it gives one power. Maybe that was why John held onto it.

Mr. John dressed all in navy blue Dickies, usually faded, and his name was stitched in cursive on the breast. His welder's cap was perched on his head. The tiny brim always faced outward from his forehead shielding no sun, smudges of ice cream and black marks from torches and rods streaking the sides. Saltcreep composed as much of the brim as the mixture of polyesters and cotton in the cap.

Allen sat in the back behind Robert. Robert reached over and handed him a large soda and his food.

Mr. John was slurping the last of his malt when Cap walked up, nodded to them, and got in.

Almost immediately Robert went out to text his father that they had a full crew and would head to the oilfields in Raleigh as soon as they had finished lunch. He asked his father what he was doing after work, if he wanted to watch the Braves and Cardinals game that night. Though seeing Cap walk up was strange, he didn't question it and didn't bring it up to Shelton.

Across town, Shelton felt the buzz in his pocket and interrupted the consultant who sat across from him. He saw Robert's message, sighed and rolled his eyes, smiled slightly, and turned the phone over on the desk without reply or acknowledgment. Shelton tried his best to listen to the technical language of the consultant for as long as he could, then ended the meeting and went home to take a nap.

Robert cranked the truck and pulled from the spot and pointed the truck north with a backward and forward jerk.

"Shit, got some on mah chin again. Take it easy there." Mr. John took the cap off, wiped his face with it and slapped it back on his head. The rest of them could not help but smile at him.

CHAPTER 4

Dani pushed the door to the kitchen closed as Jacob set himself in a chair.

"Hungry?" she asked. "*Why'd* I ask that, you're always hungry."

Jacob smiled at this and looked down in a self-deprecating, *awe shucks Ma,* sort of way.

"Vannie go home?"

"I guess so. Said that was where he was headed."

"Ms. Mora is bringing ya'll to get a hamburger later."

"Ok," he said, thinking about where his father had headed. He started to ask her, but he stopped himself. Jacob didn't want to give them a chance to argue. He figured it would come out later if it needed to. Then they could fight about it. Maybe Cap had a good reason to lie about where he was going. Maybe there was some grand plan. Cap would come home with a new mower, the kind that comes out of the box ready to use, the kind that the handle folds out like a human arm at the elbow welcoming one to use it.

"What'r you doin with the mower?" she said, walking over to the fridge and getting two slices of cheese and some butter.

"Nothin."

"Took it apart?"

"Yeah," he said, looking down. Only, this time, he was genuinely embarrassed. He knew she was mad about it. She would have to fight about it later with Cap. Jacob was already ready for school to start back so he wouldn't have to worry about it. Then they would be able to eat supper and watch television together. She never wanted to watch anything but the muted news. Jacob would eat and read the subtitles. Dani said that improved one's comprehension, and she was a teacher, so she must have known what she was talking about. But Jacob listened to her and believed her because she was his mother, not because she was a teacher. He had found that most teachers did not know what they were talking about, and it seemed they were content to be daycare workers for older kids. His mother had referred to herself as a daycare worker, that as long as the kids made it home to their overworked parents in one piece that it was a good day.

"You always take things apart. Remember the BB gun?"

"Yes."

"Then did that teach you *anything*? You're not a mechanic. Maybe one day you can work on things. Not now."

The cast iron skillet was beginning to smoke with remnants from supper the night before. Dani liked the way the remnants smelled, the way they infused and passed on taste and flavor to the next meal, cast iron genetics with a pedigree of taste. She took the butter and smeared it on and the water from it began to vaporize and fill the room with steam. She took sliced bread and laid it down and let the pieces soak up the melted butter fat before flipping them with her hand. She always burned her hand doing that and Jacob always wondered why, with a drawer full of spatulas, she continued to do that. Insanity, he'd heard, was the repetition of failed results.

A teacher had told him that.

A teacher had written it on a whiteboard.

A few seconds later, the cheese was inside the burnt slices. She turned off the cooking eye and sat down at the table. It created some anticipation. She said anticipation was a good thing. Jacob didn't know what that meant. He just knew he was hungry. He knew he could ask for half of hers when he was finished "inhaling" his. And she always gave him half. She said it was because his brain was still growing because he had to learn. She said that after age twenty the brain starts to turn to mush. She'd read it in a magazine a long time before offering the second slice to him, and he was done eating it before the smell of the grilled cheese sandwiches had left the room.

"He's gonna go crazy when he sees that thing." She had a tone, a tone Jacob always liked. It was one of deception and their working together to save Cap's feelings and a brittle peace. The tone fed her and cancelled out her guilt, at least for a little while. "Push it out to the woods in a minute. No. Do it now."

Jacob took a long drink from his water but continued to sit there.

"I said *now!*" She suddenly became stern with him. She patted the table with her hand two quick times, jarring the glasses and causing crumbs of the toast to jump off the plates.

Jacob got up suddenly with a look that was that perfect mixture of adolescent anger and laziness and submission. He smirked at her as he walked out.

"Jackass," she said in jest, shaking her head and smiling.

Jacob walked into the living room and looked out the large picture window at the pasture and the pine tree line. He could see for miles from there.

CHAPTER 5

It was a ten minute drive up to the oil fields near Raleigh. They had stopped at a gas station on the way. Cap, even though new to that crew, recognized what time wasting looked like. An old Tim Mcgraw song was sandwiched between The Beach Boys and TLC. Allen sat in the back with Cap, shoving powdered donuts and a moonpie into his mouth nearly at the same time and washing it all down with gushes of thick chocolate milk. They snaked through the backroads. As the crow flies, the oilfield was only five miles from Cap's house, but he'd gone back into town to meet them, and the roads seemed to twist and turn into a fifty mile tar and pea gravel and then clay and gravel path bypassing patches of pasture land and clay bluffs and hunting clubs and a trailer here and there.

"Gotta hook up a pipe on some wells they moved the other day. Won't take but a minute I bet, but it's a bitch ta git to," Mr. John said, then looked in the rear view. "Son, ain't nobody gone take it away frum ya!" He turned and laughed at Allen and his young face covered with white powder and milk dripping from his slick chin. "Damn," Mr. John said, smiling. "You just ate not'n hour ago!"

Cap looked out the window silently thinking about how long it would take *him* to do that weld. *John should be handing me the rods.* He thought. He looked over at Allen still eating ravenously. Allen stopped chewing when he saw that Cap was looking at him.

"What?" Allen asked.

"Nothin," Cap said then looked out the window again. As Allen finished his second lunch, he crumpled the cellophane wrapper from the donuts and crushed it without success. Aggravated, he threw the wrapper and the empty bottle of milk onto the floorboard. Cap looked down, noticing that the bag from the Drive Up was down there too, along with all the other wrappers from that week. Cap also noticed the shoes Allen was wearing, obnoxious red tennis shoes that were streaked and smeared with black tar and oil.

"What?" Allen asked again.

"Nothin," Cap said, unlacing his boots. "Take them damn things off," he said, pointing at Allen's shoes.

"You a trip Cap," Mr. John said, still wiping ice cream from his scruffy face.

"Fuckin waste," Robert said, looking back at Allen as he put on the boots.

"Just drive and drop it," Cap said, stretching his feet out as best he could in the new tennis shoes.

The truck bumped along a washboard clay and gravel road before Mr. John pointed for Robert to pull off onto a smooth tar and pea gravel thing brushed smooth with tire marks that looked like someone had been drag racing on it.

"Your turn," Robert said to Allen.

"Ain't it always Mutherfucker?"

"Yep," Robert shot back.

Cap smiled as Allen pushed with his shoulder against the door and got out and tramped through some tall grass and weeds with white daisy looking flowers and unhooked the chipped red gate made of two inch steel pipe. Allen held out his middle finger as Robert pulled the truck in slowly. Mr. John poked Robert on the arm and wheezed out a laugh and began hunting in his pocket for a cigarette.

"Goddamnit!" Allen cursed. The gate was one foot from closing. Robert had quickly pulled the gear stick down into drive and punched the gas and made the tires chirp.

"Better stop flippin off the boss's son," Mr. John offered Allen as the young man jerked open the door and jumped in.

"You all like tellin the same joke over and over and over again dawncha?" Allen protested.

"Yep," Mr. John said with the new cigarette dangling from his mouth. The flint brushed on the lighter and the older man pulled in a plume of smoke and opened the door and let it out about fifty yards down the road before he motioned for Robert to pull over. He got out and stood leaning on the hood shifting on his elbows as he took drags then blew them out, steady in his contemplation. "Pull it over there," he said as he pushed away from the truck and dropped the half smoked cigarette on the ground. He was putting it out with one foot and stepping forward with the other. Robert eased the truck into a turn around spot as Mr. John talked to them through the open windows.

"I could kill five deer every Saturday up here."

"Bullshit," Allen said as he and Robert got out.

Cap stayed in the truck for a minute, sort of as a protest, then he got out slowly and stretched his legs and pushed his pants down over his boots and scratched both of his arms across each other.

Mr. John blew smoke from the cracked window. He had gotten their permission and took care to lean his head toward the opening and held his cigarette up to flick off the ashes.

"Just one pipe?" Cap asked.

"Yep," Robert said.

"Skippy's daddy'll find us somethin else to get started on right at the end of the day. Been doin it forever," Mr. John said.

"He's shit at time managing."

"Takes longer to get started then you shut it down at five or six an set it all up again the next day. Better he thinks this takes all afternoon," Mr. John said.

"Don't put up with injuries neither," Robert said.

"You feel like tackin it on?" Mr. John asked Cap.

"I reckon."

"Backs been botherin me. I cain't lay up right now. Got too much shit to do." Cap had noticed the older man grimacing somewhat every time he would shift in the seat and when he got out to walk around and lean on the truck. Cap had figured it was just an old man with old bones that had been slowly worn down with the work over the years. Mr. John's hands were big and rough, and his face looked like an unoiled baseball glove. Covered with a tucked in shirt, his large belly contributed to the present problem. It seemed to ooze from his torso like hot taffy being drawn and looped around moving metal arms.

"What kinda shit you gotta do?" Allen asked.

"You know Brenda couldn't just pull up a trailer when that sumbitch left. Wants a *tiny* house she said." Mr. John referred to his thirty five year old daughter.

"I'd sleep on the goddamn ground 'fore I'd stay in one of them," Robert said.

"You know what I'm talkin about?" Mr. John said to Allen. "Right up your alley."

"I think it's cool," Allen said, unabashed. "Long as I live by maself."

"That ain't gone be a problem," Robert joked.

"Fuck off."

"Son, you better recognize who I am."

"Uh motherfuckin slob?"

"Ya'll knock it off dammit," Mr. John said, blowing smoke.

"Yeah, I can do it. Borrow your gloves and mask?" Cap asked.

"Yep, hope you like danglin." He smiled and looked back at Cap.

Robert and Allen laughed too.

"Goddamnit," Cap said, knowing what that meant.

EIGHT YEARS EARLIER

Ms. Armstead led the other fifteen kindergarten students through a wide hallway that opened into a carpeted auditorium. There was a puppet show set up to ease the nerves of the children while teaching them basic rules about going to the bathroom, lining up for lunch, and where to stand while waiting for the bus. The principal stood to the side in a pristine business suit with a skirt and panty hose and modest heels. She smiled as often as she could remember to remind herself. Echoes from the presentation, murmured dull sounds of people talking and children laughing were audible in the front entrance to the Seven Pines Elementary School. August sun struck through the glass and onto a bench where Vannie and Jacob each sat with a mother's arm around a little shoulder and neck. Mora and Dani were sympathetic but frustrated. Mora was late for work at the credit union and Dani's 2nd grade class was still waiting for her in the cafeteria.

"Come on boys." A little secretary motioned for them to follow her into the auditorium. It was the same secretary that Mora and Dani remembered from their time at Seven Pines years ago. Ms. Maxie was entering her 32nd year at the school and had acted this scene out more times than she could count. She took their hands after giving each one a safety sucker with paper twine embedded in hardened lime-flavored syrup. She nodded at the mothers, and the boys reluctantly followed her. The boys already trusted Ms. Maxie. They already loved her. They hugged her neck on the last day of school. They hugged her neck the first day of school the next year, and whenever they ran into her in the grocery store or in the pharmacy or the ballfield, eventually leaning down as if to pet the aging Pied Piper, feeling the curvature of an elderly spine and hearing that same high pitched giggle she would always do. In a way, Ms. Maxie had been the random Butterfly Effect for Jacob and Vannie to become friends. She had also allowed Dani and Mora to catch up on their own childhood friendship.

"This isn't right, is it?" Dani had said.

"It doesn't seem real," Mora responded.

"It makes me feel old."

"Same."

ALLEN

He was seventeen, but in every respect, a full-grown man. He got paid in cash, either from the pockets of Robert and Mr. John or from Shelton himself. Allen was a highly sought after commodity, and Shelton said as much to him many times. It was *the* reason Shelton had hired him. Shelton hired him out of the vape shop after Sera caught the kid stealing from the store. He had been selling the various items at school before and after he had forged papers to be homeschooled. He lived with his grandmother in a gray trailer with brown skirting. The brown was a mixture of paint and rust and Allen kept the flower beds pristine using money from shoplifting at Sheltons and other merchants in town. Underage people who could work and think on their feet were hard to find in that town filled with Eddie III's. Underage people also didn't worry about things like taxes, insurance, or workmen's comp. Allen could disappear and no one would know. Allen could get caught and be released for everything short of murder. His grandmother never left the house. She was senile, brain damaged, something the doctors could not figure out. Allen knew it would be a short time before he would have to send her to a nursing home or stay there full time to take care of her. But he knew he couldn't stay with her. Even with her government check, they could never afford to live without his income.

Even in that small town, Allen existed and then did not exist at the same time. Except for one thing: Allen's grandmother and Mr. John were some distant kin, far enough off to have separate Thanksgivings but close enough to be in one another's business. This was how Allen made the jump from working odd jobs for Shelton to working roustabout with the oilfield welding and fitting crew. Mr. John was teaching him to weld too.

Allen's mother was dead.

His father was in jail.

Allen's mother was more alive.

When the law passed in Colorado, Shelton noticed immediately a business opportunity that involved Allen. THC oil had been developed to use in vapor cigarettes and hookahs and such and Allen had gone several times already to buy large quantities from a man in a field on top of the flats around Denver.

Just to be safe, Allen drove slowly home on backroads. He also had a fake license and tag that would check out alright. These Shelton had made possible. The small bottles of THC were labelled as essential oils.

Shelton continued to call Allen that day and, after not reaching him, believed that the boy had gone off again to Denver. *Maybe it was to double cross him.* Shelton thought. Shelton knew when he hired Allen that this was possible, and the more he thought about it, the more it made sense to him. The boy had been talking for months about putting his grandmother in a decent home, not a government one, whatever that meant. Shelton had almost offered to pay for it himself. He could have. He hadn't talked about it with Allen yet, and by that afternoon, he had obliged himself to forget it altogether. If the kid robbed him and got away, then it would be alright. To Shelton, it was zero sum, just something to do. Either way, Shelton knew it would not be long before their relationship would be over.

He just wanted Allen to say it to his face.

Allen sat in the H.A. Smith's truck, patting his pocket every few minutes, each time realizing with a genuine surprise that his phone was not there.

THE FAMILY

They sat in a straight, unbending row. They looked like a family of four. They were unblended and unchanged by the hot sun and the hot rocks that surrounded them and the heat waves swirling up and disappearing into the air.

The father was taller and skinny, and a catwalk connected him to the other three. It skimmed alongside them like a zigzagging tether line. They were alpinists. If one held, they all might. If one fell, they might all dangle in the safety of the rope and pull themselves up and continue on. Their carabiners would make high pitched clinking and pinging sounds that would disappear like the heat waves into the air. He held oil fed directly from the well across the square, graveled yard. The two identical twins sat fat and round in between father and mother. They favored her more as they were shorter and with greater circumferences. They held the oil that would be pumped into trucks and traded on an ever-changing market. It was this market that brought the men there to open up this place and get the well back online. They were breaking its chest open like a surgeon massaging a dying heart, injecting it and rearranging it and welding it all back together to pump up the depleted blood.

Mother held the water that was taken from the children. She was shorter than them.

Father gave them oil and water and they held onto the oil.

His name was Gun Barrel.

Their names were Stock.

Mother held the water.

She took their waste and threw it out.

The waste would go away because Mother took care of it.

They sat and waited for Cap, and Mr. John, and Allen, and Robert.

LATER THAT AFTERNOON: THE DAY OF

CHAPTER 1

The picture window looked out over Mr. Pittman's pasture and to the hills farther out covered in pine trees. It was five feet tall and eight feet wide. Cap had cut it out from a smaller window as soon as they had moved in there. The window was unfinished. Wood paneling sat naked against the opening, no molding. The window sill was still bare two by material. Dani had placed little what not figurines, some ceramic birds and owls looked down at Jacob from the dusty sill.

Jacob shoved the wheelbarrow full of lawn mower parts against the house and the outside air unit. The unit rattled at him. The fan from it blew hot air in his face. He let go of the wheelbarrow and held his hand over the fan and spit into it and saw his saliva raised up and spun and tossed into the yard. Cap wouldn't see all those parts for a while. Maybe by then Jacob could get it all put back together. Then maybe Cap had gone to get a new one.

In his work clothes.

Jacob couldn't explain that.

He turned to walk back in. He wiped sweat from his face and wondered if he should cover the wheelbarrow with a tarp. But he didn't know where to find one. This would do for now.

Jacob reached the steps and was halfway in the door when he heard a thump.

He looked out over Mr. Pittman's pasture and to the state highway far off. He scanned to the left from there over the horizon of pine. Black trails slithered in the air.

His Ag teacher lived that way. Mr. Weller always talked

about burning his old tires and how it would make that same sort of smoke. He had told both Jacob and Vannie to stop by if they needed odd jobs during the summer. Maybe it was still early enough to help Weller throw some on the fire. He could give that to Cap for a new lawn mower, he thought. He could trade the old one for scrap and get more. He could pocket that. It wouldn't be much but maybe a start.

He pulled his bike out from the narrow space between his mother's car and the back wall of the garage and started off down the road toward Mr. Weller's place. Dani saw him from a window in the bedroom as she gathered sheets to wash. He was on his way to Vannie's she thought. Her phone began to buzz.

She got in the car and pulled out of the driveway headed in the opposite direction. Her mind was cloudy, and she felt high at the same time, as if she were as clear and then as desperate as she had ever remembered feeling. She never saw the smoke Jacob was heading toward. Her thoughts hid it from her. The house hid it from her. She entered into the forest canopy that almost completely blocked out the sky as she headed toward town.

She couldn't see anything then.

The Raleigh Weekly Mississippian
Obituaries
Thursday, June 7, 2006

In Memoriam †

Col. James Eden (Ret)

Services were held Monday for Col. James Eden U.S. Army (Ret) at Calvary Baptist Church where Colonel Eden was an active member and deacon. He spent thirty years in the United States Army, serving in Korea and Vietnam. He was stationed in the Philippines until his retirement in 1990. He loved his grandchildren, watching the Atlanta Braves, and hunting deer in the swamps he grew up in. He is survived by his wife Ellen, two sons, Mark (Barbara) and Gregory (Pam), both still living in Oppolusa City, MS. His three grandsons, Martin, Timothy, and Sergeant Sean Eden of Marietta, GA assisted as pallbearers. Rev. G.T. Simms conducted services at the church and at the graveside.

Robert S. Brooks

Robert Shelton Brooks has gone home to be with the Lord. He was a wonderful son and grandson. He enjoyed hunting and playing softball when he could. He was employed with H.A. Smith Oilfield Services at the time of his death. He leaves behind mourning parents, grand-parents, cousins, and many friends. He held aspirations of becoming a chemical engineer and taking on the responsibility of running his family's company. He will be interred at Town Cemetery in a private service. The family asks for privacy during this difficult time. In lieu of flowers, please send donations to Mt. Pisgah Family Church.

Mary Mclweign (correction)

In a previous edition it was stated that Ms. Mclweign's sister Elizabeth Jones of Carriere was deceased. She is very much alive and sends her regards. We apologize for the mistake.

William "Cap" Pellegrin

William Pellegrin was found deceased on June 5, 2006. He died doing what he loved most, surrounded by his friends and coworkers. "Cap" as he was known to everyone, finished his welding apprenticeship in 1990 and worked in various places including West Africa and Australia, as well as land rigs in the United States. He was a member in good standing at Mt. Bethel Baptist Church for the past twenty-five years. He enjoyed spending time with his son Jacob and tending to his walking horses. He is survived by his wife Dani and son Jacob, a sister, Sera Pellegrin, and his parents Charles and Emily Pellegrin of Graceville, Fl. Services will be held at Mt. Bethel Baptist Church on June 8th with graveside to follow at the church cemetery with Rev. Ben Whiteacre to officiate. A potluck lunch will be in the fellowship hall. A short time during the service will be set aside for friends to share stories as a tribute to Cap. Please feel free to bring a story about him to share.

CHAPTER 2

Robert pulled the truck from the small clearing they had parked in a half hour before, and in a few minutes, the woods opened up to the #9 well site. The clay gravel and the large craters that speckled the six-acre field rocked the truck back and forth. The four men shifted with it.

Mr. John winced and blew out shards of smoke as he eased himself out of the work truck in front of the four oil tanks. The largest one on the end blotted out the sun, and almost immediately, the men could all feel the temperature drop a little as the metal absorbed and released the energy.

"I'll tie you off up there on that gun barrel tank," Mr. John said.

"I cain't hang off it," Cap said, disgusted.

"You ain't gotta hang off it. Trust me. Get that ladder up there."

"Already here you old fart," Robert said from the cat walk steps. Allen followed him. Allen carried an extension ladder.

"They can put that out and you lower yourself down on it. And tack that pipe up."

Cap looked up at the tank, shielding his eyes with his hand over the small brim of the cap.

"Won't take but a half an hour. You see why we waited til now?"

"Yeah, I guess," Cap said.

Cap walked back to the truck and dug in one of the many compartments for the safety harness. He had done jobs without it before, but he figured they had plenty of time before it got dark. It was getting dark so late by then. He took it out and let his legs through and then pulled the shoulder straps over and hunted in the truck for the ropes and carabiner and looped them through. He always gave himself plenty of slack in the rope, enough to save him from hitting the ground but enough to give him room to move freely.

Robert and Allen were on one of the smaller storage tanks. They lowered the ladder down and then let it slam on the hot metal surface and pushed it across to where Mr. John had attached a clamp that would hold the safety rope. The pipe they needed to weld was shoulder high on Cap when he had lowered himself down onto the ladder.

"Fuckin stop that," Cap said sternly as Allen and Robert took turns hopping on the ladder like it was a see-saw. "Stupid sons a bitches."

"Alright Granny, *it's alright*," Robert said, holding his palm down and raising his hand up and down.

"Damn. Let me go test this," Mr. John said, stepping down from the catwalk. He took the acetylene torch off the work truck and walked it over to the large gun barrel well.

"Fuck me. It ain't cleent out!?" Cap yelled.

"It is, you know me though," Mr. John said as he rolled the oxy acetylene torch toward the large tank.

'Goddamn, ain't nothin in it," Robert hollered.

Mr. John in staccato, "Get off the motherfucker please."

They all slinked down, down the catwalk like molasses poured against the tanks in winter instead of the July day it was.

CHAPTER 3

The afternoon was passing away quickly, though the sun continued to work. It was the heat of the day when the asphalt and rocks had absorbed everything they could take. They gave it back creating a swirled haze on the horizon that Jacob could see as he rode his bike toward the smoke in the distance.

The heat rose too on the shaded pavement beneath Dani's car as she drove expectantly to meet her. They pulled into the water park at nearly the same time. Mora waved and motioned for Dani to come get in the car. Dani hesitated and mouthed out that she didn't want to sit in the car. She was nervous about it and Mora knew it. But Mora insisted with tight frustrated lips to come get in the car. Dani felt her heart beat faster. Her breathing changed. She had reached that point where she would take chances and risk things.

Risk being seen, being caught, driving toward that feeling she had come to enjoy so much and look forward to. It was a carrot dangling in front of her. She was starving. She was tired. She was tired of that feeling, expectancy, release, expectancy, release. It lasted too short a time and she looked forward to it for so long, because they had to sneak around, because they loved one another. Neither had any idea what to do with that. Many times, they would just hold one another until it got dark, risking a passerby on the road or a squirrel hunter coming in from the woods, kids on bikes.

Dani got in the car and, all in one motion, reached over and touched her behind the neck and kissed her cheek and held it there and breathed with her and smelled her. Then they drove off.

"I just left mine at home," Mora said to Dani who was turning off her phone.

Two short clicks and it was dead. They began to drive out looking for a place.

CHAPTER 4

Mr. John gave himself plenty of slack and eased over to the base of the production gun barrel well. A hatch had been opened a few days before by another crew to let the gases out. The whole place smelled of it. It was hard to distinguish if the concentrations were stronger here or there. There was no telling where the invisible stuff could be. It could hide anywhere. Mr. John had seen it before and how it looked when it all went wrong; only, it was a smaller tank that had gone up. He always flashed the tank, even if someone else had done it before. Cap offered but had been refused. Mr. John always did it himself.

He leaned with his back against the tank and held the torch in his right hand and turned the valves on. The striker flints moved against one another making a *shinkshink* sound. The acetylene flame plumed into the hot humid air.

Black and gray smoke.

Unused carbon atoms.

He transferred the torch to his left hand and turned it, extending it toward the hatch.

"Fire in the hole!!!" Robert yelled out. "Whewwwww!"

Mr. John jumped back. He dropped the torch and the flame extinguished but continued to spew the gas.

"You stupid son of a bitch!" Cap pushed Robert from the side as hard as he could. Robert fell down on his knee then steadied himself.

"Take it easy Mamaw," Robert laughed. Cap walked over and picked up the torch and Mr. John who had fallen over and was leaning against the hot tank.

"Be lucky your daddy is your daddy you cocksucker," Mr. John gurgled out.

"You better be lucky he ain't yours," Robert said smiling.

Allen stood back unfazed with the ignorance of youth.

"Turn off the damn gas!" Cap yelled at him.

The boy came to himself and ran over and turned the knobs off and took the torch from Cap.

"Ain't nothin worse than a smartass," Mr. John said getting up. "Gimme the torch."

"I'll get it," Cap said, taking the torch. He lit it and walked toward the opening. Mr. John walked behind him. Cap's left shoulder rubbed against the rough rust of the tank. Cap held his breath. He turned his body and extended the flame into the hatch.

Nothing but the dull blowing of acetylene flame and small pieces of unused carbon ribbons dancing in the air.

"I toldja it was good to go ya faggots," Robert blurted out.

A Few Years Earlier

There was no subject line, but Mora never used one anyway. It was just normal. Dani was at work, watching the students take a test. It was Friday when she clicked to open the email.

I was never good at this, so I'll just say it. I know that I risk you telling people, but I don't care. I have to tell you how I feel about things. I don't know poetry, and I think it's stupid, so I'll just tell. I look forward to seeing you all the time. I find myself wanting to talk to you more than I should, I think. The other day you took my hand when your mother said the blessing and I wanted to keep it there because I liked the way it felt. I keep thinking I ain't a dyke. Maybe I am. I don't know. I just know that I want to spend time with you. I don't care about anything else. I don't know if you feel the same way or not, and I know this will make things weird between us because of the boys, but it is the boys that make it so I get to see you, so I don't know. Please call me so we can talk about this. I don't know what else to do. I think I love you.

M.

CHAPTER 5

They walked back to their positions. Robert and Allen extended the ladder out over the space where Cap would stand, and Cap and Mr. John tied off the straps to the safety harness.

"Pussy," Robert said towards Cap.

Cap turned his shoulder and glanced and turned back quickly to the harness.

"Worthless," Cap said so only Mr. John could hear. "Why don't we drop him off on the way home. Way you did that boy awhile back."

"Just close enough so he'll walk home. Shitheap wouldn't call anybody would he?" The older man laughed and coughed.

"I was just kiddin," Robert said after getting no response.

"Gas station just above airport road?"

"Don't tell Allen. He'd let him know I bet."

"Robert needs some exercise, exercises that mouth too damn much," Cap said.

"Yep," Mr. John said as he pulled the harness tight and walked back down to get the rod. Cap was knelt down. He pulled up and down on his helmet and then took it off and wiped his face on his sleeve and blew out a puff of a sigh. He looked off into the green trees and thought that he would like to sit out there for a minute before he checked the weld later on. *Might be deerflies, maybe not though. That lawnmower, gotta get that grass cut. Boy might do it. I don't know. Dan might. She hates schoolteaching. I hate doin this, but I'm good at it. Need to get back in the circle.*

Need to call Kenny and get on with Aleutian Offshore. Get a zero turn then, hell pay Conti to do it for me. Them horses. BethAnn. Get her back at least if she ain't put down. She's in Hebron, no, Arm. I'll go see her again anyway.

"Here." Mr John handed Cap the stinger and rods. Cap looked at it and turned it over and looked at the sides and thought about his first time. He always did that, but he didn't know why. 9th Grade Ag Shop, Mr. Weller, January, navy blue coat and a fucked up weld and laughing from older boys. Cap looked back at Robert and Allen.

"You fuck around now - see what happens," Cap said, looking at Allen and Robert. The two were somewhat stonefaced at that point. Even they realized it wasn't time to play anymore.

"Hurry up man, hot as hell," Mr. John said as Cap turned and lowered himself to the ladder and pulled tight on the harness. Mr. John handed him down the stinger again then went down to pull the switch.

"Flip her on," Cap said.

The machine whirred.

CHAPTER 6

As he pedaled, Jacob remembered a few years before when he had been in third grade and they had gone to Ship Island. They were stuffed onto a sort of ferry boat that would take them to the "real beach," his mother had said. It was just the four of them, he, Vannie, his mother, and Miss Mora. They went out for the day. Nearly as soon as the boat pulled off the dock, he was able to see what he thought was the island. Vannie saw it first because Vannie always saw everything first. Jacob thought that he needed Vannie then as he pedaled looking for the smoke. The island was right there. It fooled him just like the black smoke from Mr. Weller's fooled him. Then, as he got into the trees, his vision was obscured and he became somewhat disoriented. He arrived at Mr. Weller's and there were no tires burning. *But it had seemed right there.* He thought. Just like Ship Island that Vannie could see. There were no cars, only a beat up pick up truck Weller drove to school sometimes. Then Jacob remembered that Weller was a Civil War buff who liked going to battlefields all over the place. He was probably at one then walking over the ground with his metal detector looking for minnie balls or belt buckles or swords. Weller never found anything. But that wasn't the point, he had told them. It was about trying.

Jacob pushed his body and bike forward onto the small public road. He had never been that far on his bike. Places looked different when you walked or rode a bike. Weller had said that about walking battlefields. Jacob thought to himself that he needed to find Mr. Weller when school recommenced. He would be in high school then. He would be able to take Weller's class and learn to weld, not just sit in when he could get out of class and blend in with the wall or ease back on one of the steel tables while Weller talked about welding machines and drill presses and women and the oilfield. Teaching had been his second career.

Jacob rounded a large, sweeping curve and thought he heard a car approaching, but it was nothing. He turned back to look and saw a swarm of deer flies tailing him, if there ever was a more useless creature or proof of the devil. They thrived in the shade and fed on the humid air beneath the pine tree shade. The pine straw covered the sides of the road so it looked like only one car could pass at a time, so he stayed right in the middle with the deer flies chasing him. He looked for cars in front and back. He knew there was a small rise coming. The smoke was more and more confusing. He did not realize he was getting closer and that was why he couldn't tell where it was. The tall pines made everything look strange, even the sky was not itself. He pedaled harder in preparation and built up some speed for when he would hit the small hill. It was just enough to get him nearly to the top. When the hill pushed back, he felt the pedal hit, and he forced his right leg down as hard as he could. The chain pulled tight as the bike began to work against the last ten yards of the hill. When his right leg came around again, he concentrated all his strength into it.

Then, as he reached the top, the chain broke, and all the force of his leg became free and lost in the air. His chin came down on the handlebars. His jaw let him know immediately with a sharp pain in both the sockets. He made a sudden movement and jumped with his left foot to avoid being tangled up. He and the bike fell in the pine straw.

"Shit," he said to no one. "Goddamnit!"

Cap could drive him out there the next day to get it. He should never have been that far out anyway. Who cares about smoke. He took the bike and walked it to the woods where some green, moist briars created a natural cyclone and razor fenced boundary. He picked up the bike and heaved it almost clear of the briars. In fact, it lay on them. But it blended in well. He could get that later. It was no rush.

Then he noticed, for the first time, that the roadside where he was had been scraped clean of pine straw. At least one side had been. The sound of the county tractor made sense to him then as he looked at the two sides of the road. One was clean shaven and neat while the other was still wild and sharp and dirty and tall.

LaVoy pulled the kill switch as he approached Jacob, and the thing slowly sputtered and lurched a little and died.

"You alright? Didja wreck?" LaVoy said, pointing to the bike.

CHAPTER 7

There were four tanks at Well #9. One tank, the mother, was for waste water. The father, the supply tank, held oil pumped directly from the well. The children in between were storage tanks that stored the oil taken from the supply, the oil waiting to be taken away for sale. Well #9 had been in service since the 1970's and along with the other ten wells on site, it had been a big producer for that oilfield. By the time Shelton's crew began working on it, however, it was, for the most part, a non-producing well. It was Shelton's idea that he could get it and all the other wells back online. He could harvest what was left and make more money than he'd made his whole time in business. He had already been in contact with other oilfield sites outside Mississippi. He planned on running an entire satellite business just in oil recovery from dormant wells. Then he could sell it all off or give it to his wife in exchange for a no contest divorce, ask Sera to move to Destin with him or trade her in for someone that might want to go live on the beach and drink and eat and have fun. That was all he ever wanted to do. She might want to get married. But he wasn't getting married again. It was too expensive.

Cap steadied himself on the ladder. He looked at the pipe fitting and then up at Mr. John.

"Just sit on it, be better on your knees," Mr. John offered.

"I think you right." Cap eased himself down and sat on the ladder that was rested on a small overflow pipe that stuck out from the tank and hung like a tiny limp arm in the air. "Keep it steady."

"Yep," Robert said from his own seated position.

"You all three sittin on your ass!" Mr. John laughed. "Think I might go get a bucket off the truck and have a sit too."

"Might as well." Cap's muffled voice was heard from beneath his mask.

"I'll wait til you get that tack done, I reckon."

They had flashed the tank they were working on. It had been aired out. The father was safe. The mother held the water from the well. She took the water from the father. The father gave oil to the children. The children were hiding some oil. There was oil three feet high in one of them. It was so hot, hot enough for the hidden oil to turn into an invisible and flammable vapor. Atop one of the children, the one closest to Cap and the crew, an open pipe fumed with the gaseous remnants of a dead prehistory. Everything smelled like gas. Everything smelled like oil.

So, they couldn't notice it. All Cap noticed before he yelled to them was the heat. His right leg felt like it was on fire. Then he screamed, and everything was on fire, just a small one like when he lit the acetylene torch with no oxygen. Then the fire lit the pipe, and the pipe lit the children, the tops of which were blown a hundred feet into the air.

CHAPTER 8

"My chain broke," Jacob said.

"What chain?" LaVoy asked

Jacob looked down and realized that the bike was in the woods.

"I put the bike in the woods so no one would steal it."

"Yep, everybody's wantin a kid's bike with no chain on it." He smiled.

"Did you see that smoke awhile ago?" Jacob asked.

"Can't see much in here. Somethin on fire?"

"That's why I rode out here. Heard a boom too," Jacob said.

"I thought I felt somethin, but I can't hear much when this old gal's runnin." LaVoy patted the steering wheel. "Think I might hear sirens. You hear it?"

"I think so," Jacob lied.

"I gotta little while left here. If you can wait, my trucks about a mile up the road." LaVoy pointed. "I'll take you back to your house when I'm done. If you don't wanna walk back."

"I don't even know how far that would be," Jacob said.

"Yeah?" LaVoy reached in his mouth and dug out a plug of tobacco, coughed, and spit out the remnant.

"Can I sit on the side?"

"It's my last day. You can *drive* this old bastard if you want," LaVoy said.

"Yes, sir." Jacob smiled.

"Don't get all *on* me," LaVoy protested. "Sit on the side. Just remember this old gal doesn't give a damn who you are. It'll keep on doin what it does even if your little arms get caught up or if you fall off or what a what a what."

"Yes, sir."

"You're Will Pellegrin's kid?"

Jacob winced at hearing his father's real name. No one but old people called him that.

"Yes, sir."

"I used to work with Dani's father when I was a boy. Helped him unload trucks at the wholesale place."

"Yeah? I didn't know him."

"Didn't miss much." LaVoy pushed the button and the tractor gurgled and gurgled and, just when it sounded like it was dead, it came back and moaned into a steady, high pitched roar. "Hold on," LaVoy said as he let off the clutch and lowered the bush hog.

Jacob grabbed the edge of the fender tightly as diesel exhaust and heat began to hit him in the face and blew back his hair. He watched LaVoy and the gears and tried to memorize the movements and forgot about the smoke and the boom and the pushmower.

CHAPTER 9

Annoyed, Sera crouched down in front of a set of shelves, speaking to herself.

"Shit, what was I looking for?" Then she remembered it was a promotional trifold for a new flavor that was supposed to have aphrodisiac effects. As she reached her hand in and pulled it out, the smell of cinnamon hit her in the face so hard she tasted it. "Goddamn." She took it to the front counter and opened it up to reveal a half-dressed porn star Sera thought she recognized. One smoke and they could go to bed with her. That's all it would take for life to be less ordinary.

She shook her head and set it up on the counter.

Sera took her phone from her back pocket to post a picture. She had felt it buzz and ding a while before, but thinking it was just Shelton, she didn't pay it any attention.

She began to walk in circles after seeing it, pushing her hair away from her face, the adrenaline high in her blood, her heart raced, breathing heavy. She ran out the front door to her car. She didn't leave a note. She didn't lock the door. She sped from the parking lot on her way to the oilfield.

CHAPTER 10

All Cap could feel was the heat and the wind it brought pounding at him slowly in dull bursts. Behind him, the children were on fire, the residual oil burning black soot. There was no sky, and he could see none of the crew, not one. He noticed the ladder was gone as he hung awkwardly, face against the hot metal tank, assuming he would be cooked like an egg. He yelled for Mr. John over and over again. Fire was the only answer. Fire and its low bellowed wind and the smell of oil and gas and cooked tar. He grabbed at a utility knife he always carried. But, in reaching for it, he freed himself and fell, unprepared, onto the mangled catwalk. There, he fell asleep, or passed out, for what seemed a long time. He was removed from himself, blacked out like the sky.

As he came to, he could still hear and feel the fire and the pain shooting from his hand and his leg.

He looked around but could not see any of them, and it would have been impossible to hear. Everything other than the fire was silence. Everything except that horse, and she was in trouble. Hurt from the fire too, a broken leg or worse. Cap winced from the broken leg and hand and dragged himself off the hot catwalk and onto the rocks. He followed the sound, pulling himself along the oily gravel toward Beth Ann. She was in the woods. Cap wasn't sure what he would do once he found her that would help. Maybe he could just be with her while she died.

He dragged himself the fifty yards to the woods, never turning back toward the fire. He could still hear her calling to him. He continued in, immediately feeling the coolness of the shade.

He left a trail like a giant snake from the catwalk to the woods, but the storm washed it away.

It came up quickly, the sweetness of the ozone and the cool temperature drop followed by the sound and feel of thick raindrops hitting the oilfield gravel and the fresh briars and the pinestraw and BethAnn.

He thought he could see her through the rain and through his one opened eye. Then he could feel her nuzzling his face. By that time, he was over a hundred yards into the woods.

CHAPTER 11

Outside town there was an old gas station that still had the rolling number dials on dead pumps. Sera and Shelton would stop there sometimes with one wheel of his truck resting in a large pothole by the old air hose as they both strung one another along. She used sex and attention while he used money and attention. Her car was past that place in a fraction of a moment, and still, she thought about it the whole way out there as her heart beat fast enough to kill her and her breath was in and out quick enough to make her light headed. She hadn't heard from Shelton or Cap or any of them. Sera could tell she was getting closer because the traffic was getting heavier, emergency vehicles, fire trucks, police, etc. It seemed like all the volunteer fire departments had their trucks out. Every first responder in the whole county had come out, so many that they would have to be turned away.

She was driving so fast toward it. She had to see what had happened, if Cap had been there, if he was one of the ones it said who had been "feared dead." The next of kin would be notified, but she *was* the next of kin. But she wasn't the one they would tell first. That was why she had to know for herself.

Her muscle memory, her instincts, overwhelmed her as she veered around a thirty mile an hour curve. The wheels choked on the gravel when she slammed on the brakes. Immediately, she made a u-turn, and her front tires spun rocks underneath the car and chirped a little when they hit pavement again. Not knowing what the path was like or if there was mud or if it dropped off too far,

Sera turned off the road into a hunting path. The car bobbed up and down, the suspension relenting with a whomp whomp sound. Her tires skidded on the fresh green grass that covered over the path when she braked again and jumped out and ran to Mora's car.

CHAPTER 12

The tractor sputtered and spit out chunks of grass that lined the road. Small rocks spun from underneath the housing that rolled along on a solitary pivoting wheel bereft of almost all its rubber. Jacob enjoyed the shade and the noise and the warm air from the engine exhaust and the smell of the diesel and the fresh cut grass as he thought to himself that soon it would be over and he would have to go back to school and decide whether or not to play football and then what college to go to and such.

LaVoy bumped along like he had done for years, his cap sitting high on his head as sweat beaded on his wrinkled, tan forehead, one hand perched on his thigh and the other holding tight to the steering wheel. He thought to himself that, if not for the heat, he could cut that grass for the next fifty years if he had to.

They were coming up on a small rise into a curve. LaVoy turned the tractor and lifted the bush hog until, soon, they were facing in the opposite direction.

“We’ll just go back down this way a bit, then we’ll be at my truck an they can come and get this thing tomorrow.”

“Nobody gone mess with it?” Jacob asked.

“They can try, but I’m the only one that can crank it.”

“Then who’s gonna get it back then?”

“Somebody else.” LaVoy laughed. “They’ll figure it out same as me I reckon. Best thing they could do is put some diesel on it and burn it for insurance.”

“How far?”

“Back about a mile or so from where I picked you up.”

Jacob remembered seeing the blank white single cab county truck on his bike ride up.

"Wanna steer for a minute?" LaVoy asked. Jacob reached down with his right hand and grabbed the wheel as tight as he could. The vibrations carried up his wrist and arm and even to the top of his head so his eyes began to see in a sort of zig zag pattern.

"Just keep that back wheel in line. There's a lot of slack in it, but watch you don't correct too much."

Jacob looked ahead at the road that went down the small hill and eventually disappeared in a curve and tried to make sure the cut was perfect. He had never wanted anything to be more perfect in his life, for some reason he could not figure.

"Man, I could go another ten years if you could stay and steer for me." LaVoy laughed. "You ain't gotta go back to school do you?"

"I wish," Jacob said.

"Well I might need some yard work done if you got time. That'd be work that would actchuly pay."

"Ok," Jacob responded, smiling, thinking to himself first about a new football helmet then immediately to a new lawnmower. Then maybe he could borrow one from this man. He could figure all that out later. He had to keep the line straight right then.

The county truck started off as a dot then grew larger and larger into itself as Jacob steered the tractor. His arm fell asleep from time to time, but he never took his hand off it, even when LaVoy asked him if he needed to. Then finally, when Jacob did not think he could take it anymore, he felt the machine change and looked back to see the bush hog rising, and LaVoy slowed the tractor down and pushed the kill switch.

“Welp, that’s thirty years I won’t get back!” LaVoy joked. “Now, let’s go see what all that racket an smoke’s about.”

“Ok,” Jacob said. “But I gotta get home soon.”

“Me too,” LaVoy said. “The foreman’ll be waitin on me with supper.”

Jacob wasn’t sure what that meant.

CHAPTER 13

The air conditioner kicked on and off and smelled sweet when it did. Even in the shade the air around them was hot enough to cook with. Each lay reclined in the back, captain's chair seats with a foot of space in between. Dani and Mora shared a pair of hands, fingers clasped tight so the blood stayed out. They took turns running their nails over the various rings.

Their chests were like hummingbirds' as they looked at one another.

"An you sit there and tell me you don't feel it," Mora said smiling.

"I ain't no dyke," Dani said flippantly with a smile.

"Me either."

"I feel like I might have a heart attack," said Dani. She started to tear up.

"Don't be sad. Please," Mora said.

"I just don't see a way that doesn't ruin everything."

"Maybe you could do it gradually," Mora said. Then Dani really did start. She undid her hand and began to fan herself with both palms waving in a flutter.

"I'm just very tired. I'm so tired," Dani said. "Just hold onto me please."

Mora rolled over and got on her knees on the floorboard and lay on top of her.

"I don't wanna smush you," Mora giggled.

"It's ok. I want to feel some kinda weight."

"Yeah?" Mora said, her face muffled in the seat.

"I wanna wake up with you too. I want it to be ok to see you all the time."

"Might never be that way here," Mora said.

"We can't go anywhere else. We ain't like that. The boys need their daddies."

"I know."

"What're all the sirens? You hear that?" Dani asked.

"I don't care."

"Probly kids playin with fireworks again an set the woods on fire."

"Did Jake shoot off all of his?"

"They wouldn't be up here," Dani said.

"I'm just thinkin for later. And for Mr. Pittman's field."

"Yeah, I'll check..."

Then Sera was banging on the back glass and then working her way around to the sides.

They froze.

CHAPTER 14

The community was called Covington, but everyone around there called it Cuhvie, sometimes dragging out the u sound so that it sounded as if the word hung in the air before falling out onto the ground. There were ten or so families, but those had sprung and branched from two to three larger ones, people who made their living as farmers, people who had come from North and South Carolina. Their children were farmers and loggers, and those children would be loggers and oil workers, both on and off shore, and their children would be nurses and carpenters. Some of them would move off and only return on weekends to visit retired parents and cousins. What was left was a mostly hardworking group, employed at the paper mill, teachers, contractors, and then one lady named Metz who was a migrant to that community and made and sold all varieties of goat products produced from a small herd she kept grazing around a FEMA trailer she had moved with her after Katrina. It was she who had heard the explosion first and called 911. In fact, it wasn't so much that she heard the explosion but that she felt it and then stepped outside in the heat and saw her goats running around in all sorts of strange patterns.

She was the last house on that road before the oilfield, and there was nothing past there that would make a sound like that. Everything past there was hunting land. Ms. Metz had walked that whole property and had seen every pod of wells. There were at least five of them, maybe more, surrounded by beautiful stands of pine and oak cut through by a small winding stream. It was as if someone had taken that land and hollowed it out with an ice cream scoop, leaving in place of the woods and water, divots of steel and gravel and oil slick clay. This divot was number nine. Its gate sat open. She walked up the shaded path about seventy five yards, but long before this, she could smell the burning oil. When the path opened up, she could barely make out the work truck and the four tanks. The ones on either end were blackened. The two in the middle were engulfed and their tops were opened so that both of them looked like smokestacks billowing black smoke and fire. The black smoke lifted in plumes, one after another, and she could feel the intense heat from it. To her right, she could see what looked like the top of one of the tanks. It was crumpled like paper and it smoldered at least fifty yards or more from the tanks, at the edge of the woods. The branches above the wells swayed in the rising heat. She kept looking as closely as she could to see if anything moved, but the only thing moving was those branches above her. She pulled her shirt over her face and walked closer to the tanks. The cat walk stairs were mangled and twisted and lying on the ground. It was there that she found Mr. John. There was the whooshing sound of the fire and the distant sounds of sirens and the violence of the explosion, but this man looked to be sleeping peacefully with barely a mark on him. She dropped her knee into the gravel and jabbed at him with her hand, but only his weight gave her any resistance, simply resting back after her punching at it.

Alex and Larry Taggert were first responders with the Covington Vol. Fire Dept. near Raleigh. They pulled the truck into Well No. 9 about five minutes after Ms. Metz got there. She was sitting off near the woods, breathing heavily. They both wore their painter's clothes, though Alex had been able to throw on some protective pants as Larry drove up there. They had been on ladders twenty minutes before the scanner began going crazy. Immediately, Alex began spraying while Larry looked around for survivors. Ms. Metz had pointed to Mr. John who was close to the larger tank. Robert had been blown all the way to the well itself, at least forty yards. He found Allen when he found the other top. This top had not been blown as far. It lay very near the work truck. Allen had jumped from the top just before the fire exploded the tank he and Robert were standing on, but when he landed, something happened, and he couldn't move his legs. He was attempting to pull himself toward the woods when the two tanks exploded. He saw Robert going through the black air and the top flipping like a coin. Then the second one let loose. That was the last thing Allen remembered as the flaming thing came down on him. All Larry could see was a boot sticking from underneath the steel top.

Larry walked the perimeter of the oil field and found no one else. By that time, there were four fire trucks there, three ambulances, and what looked like every law enforcement officer in six counties.

The thunderstorm came up violently and suddenly, soaking all of them, and especially LaVoy, Mora, Dani, Sera, and Jacob who had all gotten to the well at the same time. Jacob slid in the mud going up to the site, but he got up quickly and continued to run until he reached a wall of sheriff deputies.

CHAPTER 15

Shelton was home alone when he rolled over in bed. He had come home right after lunch to take a short nap that turned into a dreaming two hours. Doing things like that would have bothered him at one time, but the older he got, the more wealthy he got, he cared less and less. In there in the dark no one wanted him, no one could ask him for anything and he could experience a world of complete quiet, a thing he never experienced or ever had experienced at any time in his life, growing up in a house full of siblings who bothered him as a child and as an adult, then with their sneering and punches and noise, now with hands out and sob stories about insurance and bad jobs and the world out to "get the whites." What did it matter in his dark room? Nothing mattered. The world could die and go to hell, his own mother could die and go to hell. Maybe she had. Who cares? The low humming of the box fan blades were the only thing he ever needed to talk to, and it obeyed every time he clicked the dial.

He was hopeful it was Allen. Maybe the boy had gotten his messages and missed calls and felt guilty. Could that boy feel guilty? Shelton thought as he reached for the phone.

It was dead.

"Huh," Shelton said to himself. He raised up in the bed and rubbed his hands over his thighs still covered in the sheets and yawned. Then he heard it again, a barely recognizable ring coming from the kitchen. Then it was gone. Seconds later it started up again, and he knew it was the only landline phone left in the house. It had stopped and started again by the time he got to it.

A man's voice he did not recognize asked if it was Mr. Brooks.

"Mr. Brooks, you need to get up here to the Raleigh wells. One dun blown up. It just blowed up. Can you git up here ASAP?"

Shelton hung up the phone and looked quickly for his boots but settled for some slide on slipper shoes. He threw on a t-shirt but left his pajama bottoms on. What would that matter anyway?

CHAPTER 16

Jacob heard his mother and aunt and Ms. Mora talking, but he could not understand anything they said. The rain had let up some but still trickled on his drenched shirt and hair and pants, little pats from tiny god hands. He walked a little farther down the line until he could easily see the tanks and there was no one to stop him from walking toward them, all the lines had ended. Even the emergency personnel were just standing around waiting for someone to tell them what to do.

They were lost.

He walked past the barrier on the black, rain-soaked gravel, infinite canyons between each rock, more molecules than he could think of, many more than he could make out. It always amazed him at how easily invisible and transparent he could make himself. There was crying that he tried to ignore, crying he did not understand until he saw the steamy smokestacks and how he knew that they should not be open at the top.

The top he saw soon enough, crinkled up like a soda can. He turned to see his mother and Ms. Mora and Aunt Sera, but they were still far off.

"No!" Dani yelled. "No, Jacob, honey don't!"

He heard the crunch of rocks as he turned back to the top, and he knelt down next to it, to the boot sticking out, seeing it, realizing almost at the same time LaVoy's large hands at his back.

For years after that, Jacob would try to explain it. Everyone just wanted to know about the gore. They never said that, but they always got around to it. But no matter what he would say to them, how he would talk about the top, the explosion, the lone boot of his father sticking from underneath the metal, the other no doubt curled beneath the leg, the way his father always slept, Jacob would always talk to people about his first instinct and how he was just worried about fixing that goddamn lawn mower.

How would he put it back together?

How could they afford a new one now?

What did it matter?

What would Cap want?

What does a clamp look like?

Like a clamp, son.

What does a father look like?

Like a boot, son.

YEARS EARLIER

"Because most of the people will *not* want you there." The instructor continued his brisk then pause, brisk then pause lecture to the six students, including Molly Kay, speckled throughout the room. The young man put his hand back to a pencil and began jotting notes again, embarrassed at the obviousness of the answer.

"In twenty years with the NTSB, I saw two things. I never saw an unavoidable accident, and two, no one from the locale ever shook my fucking hand and welcomed me in. Excuse me, but that's just the way it is." He smiled at Molly Kay in a way that made her feel reassured of the instructor's knowledge but then uneasy at his language and the apology and the smile he gave her, like Ward Cleaver putting out a cigarette and then running a grey and black hand up her thigh. Why couldn't some things just be sleezy and fucked up and some things not?

"This includes the company, especially the company. The local authorities, sheriff and cops, even the victims and families won't want you there. Most of these places are industrial, blue collar. These are close knit communities that depend on what you have to investigate. They will see you as a threat even though you are there to help."

They all continued to write. Molly Kay took a second look at him, at his back and the yellow polo shirt and the tan slacks and tennis shoes that looked out of place as he got to the front of a row of desks and turned.

"But you aren't there to be their fucking buddy. You're there for the next guys. You're there so it doesn't happen again. If anyone tries to stonewall you, just show em the warrant. That works ninety-nine of the time. If it doesn't, just leave and call your supervisor. *Do not* confront anyone. Don't *ever* do that." He walked to his podium and turned a dial. The lights became dim as the OSHA emblem reappeared on the drop screen. The solemn piano intro began to play as they all watched and took notes on yet another industrial horror story.

Molly Kay looked over her notes from earlier, pages flipping, rustling, her pen running over it as she struggled to see in the dark a small rectangular doodle of a camera and her quote of the instructor. "It's all digital, take as many pics as you need to."

FOUR DAYS AFTER THE ACCIDENT

CHAPTER 1

"I don't understand," Jacob said, pushing his back against a treated fence post, bracing himself against it so that the attached panel stayed plumb or close to plumb.

"Whatchew don't understand?" LaVoy asked.

Jacob dropped the fence a little then backstepped to get it back to level. "I don't understand why you need a privacy fence. There ain't no one around here for like two miles."

LaVoy heaved the concrete bag over to the hole and let it drop to the ground. The impact broke it open just like he planned, and the dust cloud plumed up into both their faces. He took a garden rake turned upside down and packed the concrete down in the hole a little then sprayed water down in the hole until he was satisfied it was enough. Then he poked the rake in the hole, punching it up and down again.

"Well it ain't me that wants it." He pointed his thumb back inside and smiled.

"Oh," Jacob said.

"Watch out," LaVoy said as he reached under Jacob's shoulder and propped up a two by four. "Now you can move."

As Jacob moved away, he noticed that the fence stayed put.

"Then what did you need me for?" Jacob asked confused.

"I guess I didn't, Donut Head."

"What?"

"Nothin." LaVoy smiled. "I needed somebody so if I fall out they could call 911, but you probably ain't that good in math."

"I am too," Jacob shot back.

"Then tell me this, if a train leaves Bogalusa at twelve and another train leaves Hurricane Creek at twelve, which one'll get to Bassfield first?"

"How far is it to Bassfield?" Jacob asked.

"About forty miles as the crow flies."

"And how fast?"

"They both are going about 45 miles per hour," LaVoy said. Jacob looked down, wiped his dirty face with a dirty, sweaty forearm, then looked up quickly.

"I think the one comin from Hurricane Creek."

"Wrong."

"How so?" Jacob asked like a trial lawyer.

"There ain't no station in Bassfield no more, an never was one in Hurricane Creek to begin with."

"That's bullshit," Jacob said, disgusted.

"Yep, most of it is anyway." He slapped the boy on the arm and pulled Jacob up with him toward the front porch. They both sat down on the top step. LaVoy pointed at the fence.

"See that, now no one can see us on the porch til they're right in front of the house."

"Why?"

"Don't matter why."

"Whatever," Jacob said.

"How long you been out here?"

"About three hours."

"You ain't Union are ya?"

"What?" Jacob said in genuinely perplexed.

"Nevermind. Here's forty. Should be thirty, but I bet you ain't got a ten on you."

"Nope."

"Then I guess you owe me another hour or so."

"I reckon," Jacob said.

"When you wanna do it?"

"What else you got to do?" Jacob asked.

"Son, I've got about thirty years worth of Honey Do's to take care of, and all she's got to do all day is sit up at that central office and make lists. As they would say, the possibilities for employment are endless."

"This stuff you gonna need me on, or stuff you just wanna pay me for callin 911?"

"Both."

"You ain't gotta babysit me," Jacob said.

"I ain't never babysat nothin in my life. I don't reckon I'll start now," LaVoy laughed.

"What about your own kids?"

"Ain't babysittin when it's your own."

"What about grandkids?"

"Ain't got none of those yet, but I would think they fall into the same category."

"It was a good funeral wasn't it?" Jacob said.

"You don't have to say that."

"But that's what people say."

"It's what old women say when they think they need to talk about somethin that doesn't have to be talked about."

"I don't wanna talk about it then."

"That's just fine. It was a damn shame. We can say that."

"It was a damn fuckin shame," Jacob said.

"Don't say that around my wife. But that's exactly what it was."

"Do they know what happened yet?"

"Think the tank wasn't empty but it was supposed to have been."

"What was in it?"

"Oil."

"Oil dudn't explode."

"Does when it's a gas," LaVoy said quickly. "Gets hot, makes a gas. Touch a torch to it, it's like a rocket. You see?"

"Yeah. He was a good man."

"You don't have to say that either."

"I know."

"He was just a man," LaVoy said.

"He was mine though, I guess," Jacob said, somewhat abashed. "Can I still borrow your mower?"

"Yep. We'll load it up and I'll drop both of ya'll off. When's your mom off work?"

"She ain't at work really. Just went in to fix her class up, just workin in her room."

"I guess it pays to stay busy."

"I don't know if she's gonna go back."

"What'll she do?"

Jacob frowned and shook his head. "I don't know. She said we might move somewhere, but I don't want to."

"Where to?" LaVoy asked.

"My grandparents had a place; the house is still there just rentin out. She said we could go there and sell our house here."

"Good luck sellin a house out here."

"Yeah?"

"Yeah," LaVoy said.

"It was a good funeral."

"Yeah it was," LaVoy said absently.

The old man got up and grunted. His knees popped and he cracked his knuckles.

Jacob noticed that older people made a lot of noise.

"Let's get that mower over there before it gets *real* hot." LaVoy laughed and wiped his forehead and set his cap back on his head and started to walk around to the back of the house for the trailer and the mower.

Jacob sat for a second looking at the fence, tilted his head a little to the side, then remembering himself, he got up and followed the old man. While LaVoy was getting the keys inside, Jacob went to the car house.

The car house shed sat with two open bays, one empty except for some tools stuck handle down into five gallon buckets and some hay haphazardly scattered across the dirt floor. The dirt floor was tinted a green that Jacob could see underneath the shallow straw covering. The place smelled like cut grass and a faintness of mildew, but it was cooler in there, so he didn't mind it. It reminded him of their barn only smaller. He could hear LaVoy cursing in disgust and thinking that the boy couldn't hear. Jacob stood looking at the walls of the car house and at the tools and the jars full of nails that sat along the edges of two by fours nailed parallel to the ground. It smelled like their barn too. Jacob thought about what would happen to it. What would the next person do with that barn? Live in it? Bulldoze it? Maybe he could come back one day and buy it, but then what use would he have for that town. What use would it be to come back? There was a rectangular block of wood sitting upright and Jacob walked over and sat on it and took a bamboo stick leaning against a post and began to poke at the straw and the dirt. The divots started out in a small pattern like a tight twelve-gauge shotgun might make. Then it got larger until he had pockmarked a space of at least five square feet. He would poke then turn, poke then turn again, always clockwise like a tightening screw.

Suddenly, it hit something solid. The bamboo had split at the end and caught the metal screw clamp, flipping it over. Jacob leaned down and picked it up, spit on it and rubbed it with his thumb.

"Looks like a clamp son." Jacob remembered his father saying. He realized that maybe this was what he had been looking for. Cap had known so much, and Jacob didn't even know what a clamp was or if this was the right one or even how to put a mower back together. He threw the clamp toward the back of the car house where it hit against a tin wash tub and made an impotent, hollow pop. Then he began to stab the bamboo into the dirt again, each time breaking the stick until he was leaned over and pushing the ever-shrinking bamboo to the ground. When it got to be a foot long, he stopped, stood up, and threw the stick too. Then he sat back down and began to rock with his arms crossed and he knew it was starting all over again and he knew once it got going he couldn't stop it. But he figured that if a person couldn't cry for their daddy or mama then what good were they. It seemed to start in his feet and work its way up as he rocked, and by the time it got to his brain he was making enough noise that LaVoy could hear him as soon as the old man got through the back door. He walked or ran as fast as he could across the small back yard to the shed and instinctively pulled the boy up to him. LaVoy felt tears seeping into the shoulder of his shirt as Jacob stood on the wood block sobbing something inaudible to the old man. Jacob went on for several

minutes. LaVoy apologizing several times for leaving Jacob alone, then it went back down from his brain and oozed from his feet. He felt better. He got past that part where he thought it was a dream and the realization it was not.

"You still wanna load it up, or wait till next time?" LaVoy asked.

"Let's go ahead and do it."

"I can come out and cut it myself."

"I wanna do it," Jacob said.

LaVoy walked over and cranked the truck and pulled it around like he'd done a million times before, feeling it out through muscle memory like an old catholic with the rosary or a guitar player pressing chords with closed eyes. Without any help from Jacob, he put the ball directly under the trailer hitch and directed the boy to crank until the tongue fell, then he jumped out and jammed in the pin. LaVoy put the small single cab in gear and the two things seemed to jump from the yard together. They bumped along the county road to the highway and stopped at a station to get drinks and put some gas in LaVoy's metal can. The old man lurched his train toward the highway and put his blinker on to take a right when another truck, muddy and dusty all over, flew past the station with its flashers on, creating a small turbine wind in the dirt and gravel lot.

"Somebody's in a damned hurry. That a company truck?" LaVoy said.

Jacob nodded that he thought it was as he looked down the road.

"CSB. You seen it before?"

Jacob shook his head.

"Hope they don't kill nobody drivin like that," LaVoy

said as he checked again and pulled the truck onto the highway.

CHAPTER 2

Dani and Mora met at the side door of Dani and Cap's house, the former still unstrung but feeling a little more level and warm with each sip she was taking from a stemless wine glass. There were signs that she'd spilled some on her pajama bottoms. Her dark hair roots were beginning to show amongst the blonde sago palm plume pulled in a tight band atop her head. Dani said nothing, just nodded and opened the door and smirked. Mora understood what that meant. *The house was a mess and who gave a shit.* Mora walked in and shut the door. Dani set her glass down carelessly on the counter.

"They're gone to Leatha....." Mora tried to say that Vannie had gone with his father to her in-laws for a few days to fish, but she was interrupted by Dani's embrace. She pushed her face into Mora's neck and Mora thought that she felt lips as Dani tasted the salt of summer sweat and held her hands tightly against the folds of Mora's skin over her bra. She pressed her fingers there and felt herself being carried farther and farther away. Then Mora felt Dani's head move and their teeth clashed together a little as they tasted one another's mouths in that awkward way that first times are. It had always been Mora that had been the more daring one, the one who had wanted this to happen, but here it was Dani who pulled Mora to the couch in the living room. Mora had been dressed from work, but she had gone home and put on a t-shirt and shorts before coming over. She pushed her tennis shoes off her feet as she laid down on top of Dani and continued to kiss her and tasted the wine and felt the wetness of the tears that still moistened both of their faces. At that point, Mora did not care why Dani was pulling harder. It didn't matter. It would always be that way, where one thing worked harder than the other. Then the world would move and change again.

They had seen one another naked so many times that there was no mystery in it, but for the first time, they touched one another and felt one another and heard one another in that way. And there was no rushing off to the bathroom or falling asleep when it was over. In fact, it felt like it was never over, that there was only the interlude of reality, the sounds of cars passing on the road or Pittman's mooing cows in the pasture and the buzzing of the window unit in the kitchen.

"Just four or five more years and the boys'll be gone, and we could move off and be whatever," Mora said, rolling herself onto her back on the carpeted floor.

"You remember that Collins kid was their age moved off?" Dani asked.

"What happened to his mama?"

"Still in jail I think."

"That went on for two years and the social worker knew about it. They didn't do shit."

"She oughta be in jail her damn self," Mora said.

"I could get a masters in that online."

"Better job than that cunt."

"Yokona. That's where I want to go."

"Where?" Mora asked.

"Little place, near Memphis."

"Why in the hell you wanna go to another small town and live?" Mora laughed.

"Not live, just visit. My daddy had family there. My Mamaw was there. Used to go stay there just before school got started. I wanna live in Memphis, or some other place big."

"Mine was in Corinth Crossroads. I need to lose about twenty pounds."

"Livin in the wrong place fur that," Dani said.

"I wanna walk through Corinth, go to Shiloh Battlefield."

"You could lose forty pounds in the heat."

"Daddy went ta every damn battlefield in the South. If he had a three day weekend, that was where he'd go. Just him and his little pug mix and a jug of water and a Shelby Foote book. He lived in Memphis."

"Shelby Foote's dead?"

"Not long after Daddy. That whole book Daddy had is full of pictures and drawings and places he camped out with that goddamned pug dog."

"I might like that," Dani said.

"Why is it that we only care about dead people?" Mora stopped herself and listened to the silence for a second before shooting up to where she could see Dani's face. Mora rested on her elbows.

They locked eyes with one another, but where Mora expected to see tears, there was nothing but a gaze, a stare.

"If I never cut another blade of grass..." Dani said.

"I want a condo, a balcony full of dead plants," Mora followed.

The two laughed.

"I wonder what it's like not to give a shit about anybody for a while?" Dani asked.

"Ask that social worker."

"Four years?"

"Five years. Maybe four. But then maybe only three years of so after that. The boys'll be pumpin out soccer players and ballerinas not long after." She grinned.

"Yeah." Dani smiled too. "I guess I can always start reading books again. I used to read all the time."

"I remember. You know you can listen to them just as easy now."

"Uh huh." Dani nodded and then turned to the sound of LaVoy's wheels in the driveway.

"I can't believe he didn't wanna go fishin with Vannie and Shithead."

Dani's phone began to vibrate and beep on the coffee table. Without looking, Mora handed it to her.

The grated iron tailgate of LaVoy's trailer swung down and lashed against the gravel, echoing through the house and startling them both.

CHAPTER 3

Shelton was on his way to find Allen when he passed the strip mall. Seeing the OPEN sign flashing at his shop, he couldn't wait until he reached the intersection to make the turnaround. The tires screeched as he jammed the brake and spun the wheel. The suspension made it feel like a giant mechanical water bed, easy and flowing as the truck lurched back into the parking lot and pulled sideways into a spot next to Sera's car, still mud spattered from her drive to the oilfield a few days before.

She had on her customer service face, her customer service smile and tone when the door toned, welcoming and congenial and helpful. Then, when she saw Shelton, it deflated and condensed into a heavy wedge, a butcher knife striking a rock.

"Yep," she said flint-faced, busy and preoccupied.

"Honey, you don't need to open. Just let it be and come back in a week."

"Thanks Dad, but I can get it. Who else is gonna run it, you?"

"It can stay closed."

"And deliveries?"

"I'll get somebody," Shelton said.

"Who, Allen?" she shot back.

"I'm workin on that right now. May have to go on a little road trip to find my little buddy."

"You make it sound like he ain't a grown man that carries a pistol everywhere he goes."

"He ain't got the balls to.."

"Who does?" she asked.

"I'm gonna go ta Colorado and find him."

"You think he's with John Elway? How you gonna find him? You been by his house?"

Shelton suddenly realized he hadn't been, that he hadn't even thought about doing that. Suddenly he composed himself, or tried to. "I was, I was on my way there right now."

"Really?" She looked up from a box she was opening. "You're so fuckin stupid. Let me tell you, if you do find him, tell him he's fired, from everything. Everything, you hear me?"

"You wanna?...."

"Everything!" She slung the box across the room and ran to the back office and slammed the door behind her.

Shelton sighed and walked to the front door and unplugged the sign. He turned the metal bolt and walked to the back office. He put his hand on the door and tried as hard as he could to speak softly.

"Just come with me, it's pretty up there."

She always kept one of her old aluminum softball bats in her office. She picked it up and tried as best she could to aim where she thought his hand was flat to the cheap pressed cardboard door.

"Stop talkin ta me like I'm a little girl!"

"Damn!" Shelton stood back holding his hand. "Shit!"

She began to hit him in his bare fat arms with the bat, not enough to break but just enough to get his attention. She knew which was which and she continued to strike or attempt to strike him with each syllable.

"I sent him out there! Me! Dontchew care about shit!? Robert? Robert!"

"*I do. I do,*" Shelton relented.

"I do. I do," she said, mocking him. "I do care about pussy and money and booze."

"Honey, I, I think you need to settle down and take a week..."

"Get the fuck, get the fuck away from me. I'll kill you if I see you again!"

"That dudn't even make any sense now. Come on," Shelton said.

"Just wish they'd had take your daddy ta work day." Shelton had backed up to the door. From behind his back, he undid the lock and began to let himself out.

"We'll finish this. We'll talk when I get back."

She slung the bat like a propeller across the floor of the vape shop, taking out two displays. As his truck cranked, she plugged in the sign and went back to work.

As he rode along the highway toward Allen's trailer, the sky was dark and bruised looking with light rays shooting from underneath the outer boundaries of the clouds. Shelton remarked to himself how he always liked a good summer thunderstorm. He liked it for what it reminded him of, of sitting on a wood porch with his grandmother while she shelled peas, of feeling that sudden temperature drop and the wind and the specks of water that would blow in and hit him in the face as he tried without patience to shell his own small bowl.

Any second, he thought, the rain would begin to fall in big heavy drops against the windshield. He set his hand against the glass and felt the coolness and the way the truck was rocking back and forth in the cross wind.

As he turned onto Allen's road, a little side street that sat along the edge of the bypass, he could see the boy's car and the back glass, dirt etched with curse words the neighbor kids were always putting there, marks of passing time, *fuckin fagit fucker* in tiny handed, artistic graffiti. As if answering his wish that the rain would hold off, all of the sky opened and vomited out enough water to soak him before he got to the porch covered with a tin roof and lined with lawn chairs the grandmother never used.

The old woman weighed about 70 pounds, and she was rambling around the house in a jerking fashion, her face moving from side to side in sudden movements yelling at Albert to get ready for work.

"Miss Dilsy, Albert's in jail," Shelton advised.

"Allen's in jail. Allen's in jail," she said quickly, walking over to a small toaster with a mitten on sleeving her hand. She reached the toaster and looked at it intently as smoke began to subtly fume from the door. She looked at the smoke and seemed to be concentrating on it heavily, then she looked up at the detector that was still hanging by a single wire from the popcorn ceiling. She looked back at the toaster and the smoke and took off the mitten and picked up a griddle from the counter. Shelton was amazed at how precise she was as she aimed and squinted like a carpenter with a nail and hammer before knocking what was left of the smoke detector onto the floor. Then she shuffled back toward the side of the house where Allen's room was. Shelton quickly ran over to the toaster and yanked out a tray full of black charred oyster crackers.

"Albert! Albert! They gone fire yo ass!" The old woman was yelling from the back room. By that time, the whole open kitchen and living room was filled with smoke. The rain had not let up. Just then, a dog came running in through a hatch in the back door, a stout walker hound mix that loved and nuzzled Shelton when Allen would bring him around. When he saw Shelton, the hound began barking and peeing, first at the kitchen table, then at Shelton's feet. He bent down to pet the dog, but it was so excited that it continued to roll over and over and slurped at Shelton's legs. Shelton put up with it for a minute, but the sounds of loud barking and the yelling of Ms. Dilsy who had turned on the television to a midday news show, and the hammering rain on the tin was about to cause him to have a breakdown. He stepped out on the porch to alleviate some of the noise. He took a handkerchief from his pocket and wiped his face and tried to breathe a minute and think.

He walked back in and in five violent seconds had turned off the tv and thrown the dog into the back yard. The rain was still hammering when he walked back over to an unmoved Ms. Dilsy who was eyeing the toaster oven again.

"Where's Allen?" he asked.

"Allen better get to work too when he gets out," she said. "He's gone ta the jail."

"Shit!" Shelton yelled as he got back up and walked heavy-footed to Allen's bedroom. The room, in fact the whole house, was pretty well ransacked looking already, so he began to go through the drawers that were still in the dresser and the ones on the floor too. The closet was empty except for a lamp lit over two small marijuana plants. He stuck his hand in the soil and felt that it was dry. He had been leaning over with his hands on his knees, but he bent down and plopped himself on a small mound of dirty clothes and sat there listening to the rain and the grandmother shuffling again. Shelton knew that Allen always took that dog with him when he went to Colorado, and he never left his grandmother alone without a cousin being there or paying a girl down the road to sit with her if he was out for too long.

He always answered Shelton's calls and texts. Shelton sat for several moments as the rain pattered on the trailer roof. Shelton wasn't sure *where* it was in the room, but he knew it was there, as he held his phone out after dialing Allen's number. He waited a second, then he could hear the rhythmic buzzing, maybe somewhere underneath the bed or in the window under a pile of senior care brochures and used paper plates. The sound came to a high frequency climax then stopped, like droplets of water turning to steam on a hot pan.

CHAPTER 4

The late afternoon Sun was bright hot reflecting off the gravel and red clay. The H. A. Smith work truck sat baking in the distance, all the tools left from days before. Some traces of blood could still be seen in the gravel, and especially where the top had come down, where Jacob had seen his father's boots. And that shirt was still fluttering in the tree above her, waving to her like an ominous, vulture-like thing. Every once in a while, the wind would offer a short reprieve and blow some dust across the drying ground of the oilfield. Molly Kay had no service on her phone, but sometimes a text would come through, or several all at once. She had gotten four from her father but only one from her mother. Her mother was a cat, classy and independent, loving and strong and solid, while her father filled the role of romantic ne'er-do-well, a Hemingway without the talent.

The aluminum ladder was broken into pieces, small fragments were scattered around the gravel. No matter how many pictures she took, it seemed that a piece of the ladder Robert and Allen had been standing on would find its way there, as if peeking out from the side saying "*Don't forget I was there too.*"

The chains Cap had been hanging from gripped part of the ladder, giant things dangling from the clamp atop the Father Tank, holding onto bits of crinkled shiny metal rungs. She resisted the urge to touch the chains and knock loose the rungs and hear them clang. The cord from the stinger Cap had been holding was interlaced also with the chains and was frayed crazily at the top like one of those cheap carnival prizes, a flashlight with glowing plastic protrusions.

As she walked around the tanks, she found and photographed a company net cap, Mr. John's seemingly untouched and as peaceful as the old man had been when Ms. Metz found him near the fire. "H.A. Smith Oilfield Services" it read across the front in that same blue Shelton had painted on all the company trucks when he took over. Around behind the children tanks, she took note of the way the bolts were buckled and how the bases of both tanks were bulged like a soda can left too long in a freezer. She saw the small projection, that one thing like the finger of Adam in Michelangelo, that one thing that connected the Father and Children, one a symbol of creation, and then this thing, what was it, dank and sad and lonesome hot, thick hot. There was the opening to the empty Father, a square bolted all around, pipes everywhere lay strewn, not from the accident but just from the daily work of the well that Shelton was bringing back to life.

A shoe sole.

A sign that warned about open flames within 50 feet.

The Welder's mask empty of an artist.

Baked, a million shallow clay encased footprints, unable to tell the living from the dead.

She climbed what was left of the catwalk and took pictures of the peaceful skim of oil in the first child, peaceful in the earth for millions of years, pumped up and sacrificed and unleashed in all its explosive energy, and there was no way to get around it, as she clicked through the photographs checking them, she could see her face hidden by a camera reflecting in the pool below like some sick serenity pond.

Only the sounds of the woods accompanied her as she worked, and she could see out in the distance the top of the second child that had been blown completely from the field, more than a hundred feet from its source. She continued, snap snap snap, as she walked gently down the stairs and back behind one of the children, just above where a closed but leaking hatch sat, she stopped and stared for a long time at a spray paint drawing, a stick figure of a little curly haired girl smiling away, completely unaffected.

She began walking past the family of four to the well itself and took several more pictures before continuing on into the woods toward the top.

It was brown and rusty like everything else, but with black bars of oil cooked onto its surface in randomly repetitive patterns. It lay across a patch of green briars, the kind with stalks as thick as a dime and sit lush and soft waiting for something to catch. She struggled against the thicket that pulled at her arms and legs and left what seemed to be hundreds of small shark teeth travelling on her clothes. It was as if a god or a giant had taken the top of the tank and squeezed it gently between thumb and index finger, bending it slightly and then tossing it like a coin so many hundred feet into the air, arcing away and then toward the hot earth of the oilfield.

Molly Kay kept looking back at the well and the family of the well and the shirt that furled and furled in waves with every subtle breeze. She had seen many accidents since leaving her certification class, but this was the first where loss of life accompanied that of mere property, and not just a single person, but three. She tried not to think about it, each time beginning to take pictures again. What did it matter if there were duplicates? It didn't. She must have taken fifty pictures of that shirt in the tree, and this top would be the last thing. She could truly say that she had taken account of everything. Besides, Manuel would be by in a day or two and do the same thing. It was protocol.

She returned to the truck and put the camera in the passenger seat and sat with one leg on the floorboard and the other on the ground and took a moment to think. Maybe one day this would be a routine occurrence and she would be unaffected, like an emergency room doctor or a human services agent with the State. One day, none of this would matter. She had heard her father talk about "crusading days" and how that would stop eventually, that either people burn out and quit or just stop caring, but he worked in a bank so she wasn't sure what to make of his thoughts. Maybe it made sense. But being crusading days, or whatever one wants to call it, something made her turn onto that fire lane to see if anything else had been blown farther than the top. The oilfield butted up to 16th Section land and LaVoy himself had mowed down the fire lane surrounding the timber land a month before the accident. Already the briars and trees had begun to overtake the lane as Molly Kay pointed the hood of her truck onto it. Except for the heat and pine trees, it reminded her of home, fields encased by hardwood forest that she and her brother would play in until it got too dark to see. She looked at her watch and thought that it would be nearly dark back home. But here, the Sun seemed to fight harder to stay alive.

CHAPTER 5

He would have stopped in by now, Sera thought to herself. And he would be criticizing the coffee's age and staleness and she would tell him exactly what she thought of his opinions in explicit detail. She fixed the second "E" with the black paint marker as the chemical smells filled her nostrils and choked her out a little so that she did a weak sort of throaty cough. The phone buzzed on the counter again. Without looking at it, she picked up the second piece of poster board. She had walked down to the other end of the strip mall to the dollar store to get the boards and the paint marker an hour before. When the phone buzzed again, she picked it up and squeezed the button to power it off. A little glowing circle chased itself around and two quick dings let her know she had killed it.

She started on the I or the E. She cursed for having to look up such a simple word, then she cursed again for having killed the phone. It was definitely an I.

"Inventory."

She started in with the paint marker and began to cough again.

When they were kids, she and Cap would go down to the lady at the end of the road and steal popsicles from an outdoor deep freeze. Sera would always try to grab more than one, sometimes three or four. Cap would make her put those down so there would still be some left for the next day, sometimes clutching her wrist and shaking until the popsicles tumbled back into the cold smoke.

And that's what she was doing. She felt like she had taken too much. Sera looked down at her right wrist and thought she could feel him shaking at it all over again, so that in some small way, she was throwing something back into Ms. Quentis' deep freeze.

People started in at first in a suspicious trickle, wondering if it was really so, then when they saw that it was, a crowd began to gather.

Within an hour, everything in the store was gone, even the computer in the back office, the chair too.

Sera latched the glass front door, then went to the back and put the key in the deadbolt, pushing at the metal door hard with her knee to get it to catch. She stood back for a second, looking at the molded white cinder blocks behind the vape shop, up to the eave where two butted against one another were broken.

It took a few tries, the key pinged back and fell in the gravel until finally she found just the right angle and arc and the key fell sweetly into that triangular crevice with one final high-pitched ring.

CHAPTER 6: THE LAST CHAPTER

Just as Molly Kay turned onto the backside of the fire line, an oak limb scraped across the hood and windshield. The wheels locked and slid in the grass and mud mix of the path, and the truck slid a little before stopping.

It looked like a deer, but flat and somehow darker and still. She turned the truck off and sat looking at it over the dash, then all at once, the middle rose and a gutteral sound of inhalation filled the empty forest around her.

Immediately, she jumped out and ran to him and rolled him over on his back. A high pitched whine came from deep inside. She ran back to the truck and grabbed her phone, constantly talking to Cap and telling him things, perhaps inaudible things, of reassurance. When she got no signal on the phone, she threw it back in the truck and fell down on the ground behind him. She could tell that both of his legs were broken by the way they fell around him. Molly put her arms underneath him and began pushing with her legs, frantically full of adrenaline, unaware that she was tearing her own skin. She was to the back of the truck with him in a few minutes. Her father had taught her how to get a deer in the back of a pick up when she was a kid, and she used the same method with Cap, wrapping a flannel shirt around his torso and under the arms and pulling him onto her back from a squatting position and then pushed him into the truck bed flat on his back again, tucking the broken legs in at grotesque angles like the man was a rag doll. He seemed not to object at all, but kept on with the hollow breathing, his last struggle to live.

She paid no attention to how hard or fast she drove, and as soon as they jumped onto the highway, she began calling 911 and searching for a map to the hospital.

She checked on him constantly in the rear view.

Somewhere in his partially conscious mind, the darkening sky played out overhead like an infant's mobile. The one eye that would, opened and closed as if to signal a change in scenes. Beneath his back he felt the rumble of BethAnne as she carried him off.

His fingers weakly gripped the reins.

Somewhere in his mind, he pulled BethAnne to a stop and swung his leg over and began leading her to the stable. He was patting her on the head when the doctor shined the light in his face, gripped his oily, burned black cheeks, bringing him back to life where he would stay.

Cap let loose with a groan, his open eye wild and wide.

READ MORE FROM THIS AUTHOR!

AN EXCERPT FROM

JIMMY FORETTE: A SHORT NOVEL

There was a main intersection in the town that had once been a muddy trail for horses and wagons, then there were cars and trucks, lots of cars and trucks, so many cars and trucks that the stop signs were replaced with traffic lights. It stayed like that for a long time, then people started moving to other places, finding jobs elsewhere, had fewer kids, fewer cars, fewer trucks. The traffic lights were taken down and replaced once again with stop signs, only this time, the signs were a shiny red color, with decorative iron posts holding them.

Jimmy Forette walked toward the intersection, not on Main street but a side street, News St. He walked past the florist and waved through the windows of flowers to a lady he did not recognize but who *did* recognize him. He walked past the funeral home and remarked to himself about the iron scroll work on the front porch and remembered how he had stood on that same porch as both adult and child, staring out down the street and over part of the town. The building sat high on a mound of earth. Outside the dry cleaners, there were several workers leaning against the concrete sides of the building. Two were smoking and blowing out clouds, another was taking a phone call. All of them nodded or waved when he walked by as he did likewise. Jimmy noticed that he waved with a different hand than before, with his left hand, across his body uncomfortably. He decided it would be a good idea to shift the brown sack he was carrying to his left hand, but regardless, he did not think he would have to wave at anyone again before he reached the intersection. The next two businesses on News St. had closed a long time ago, but it didn't bother him much. There were other places to get hardware and buy clothes, but he felt it was a shame regardless.

He had on faded blue overalls and the rivets were getting hot from the Sun, burning the tender parts of his arm as the weight of the bag forced it close to his hip. From then, only a block, he carried the bag out from his body. He hoped to himself that his posture looked as awkward as it felt. He reached the corner where the clothing store had been. There was nothing there now, but since the clothing store left, there had been a temporary tax service and a cell phone outlet in that building, the latter leaving its orange mark in several wavy swoops across the brick exterior. His dark boots reflected an opaque Sun as he waited for the car to stop before he crossed the intersection. His hands were dirty, and his shoes were dirty. His whole outfit was dirty. The driver of the car seemed to notice this because she looked at him strangely, wondering, it would seem, just why a man of Jimmy's age would be walking out in the hot Sun when he could be doing any number of other things indoors: watching television, sleeping, sleeping with the television on. She had summed him up, just as Jimmy had summed her up, single mother, two kids in the car, her mother's car probably, taking tens of dollars from his check every month in the form of welfare, food stamps, kids' medicine she couldn't afford. He knew who she was just the same as she knew him. Most likely, both of their predictions about the other would have been true, reinforcing that stereotypes exist for a reason. She was gone out of sight very soon after he saw her and the car. He was sure he knew who she had been or could find out easily, but what would be the use in it.

News St. was divided into a boulevard on both sides of Main. There were a few trees that took up the median and there were several spots where a car could turn around. It went in a fairly regular pattern, except for the Doughboy House that sat square in the middle of the boulevard. The house was built in 1904 and served as a meeting room for the Oddfellows and later, the Chamber of Commerce. During the day it was a sort of meeting place where men would tie up horses and talk and pass the time, share a bottle while their wives shopped. It also served as a Post Office, then later as a train station, and then as a bus station. During World War I, when it served as a train station, the soldiers would come by to get their tickets for the train ride to New Orleans. So many of them showed up at the same time that a fight started between draftees pushing in on one another. Several of the windows in the building were smashed, as was the front door. The town police responded by writing tickets to every single soldier there, making an allowance that the ticket would be torn up when the violator returned and helped fix the damage. While they were gone, the building was left just as it was, people working around the damage for a year and a half, when most of the soldiers returned. The tickets were ripped up, the place was fixed. There were twelve tickets left over. These were pinned up and shellacked into the wood wall of the building, and that is how the Doughboy House got its name. Aside from that, it is important to know that the building Jimmy Forette sat outside of, on the lone bench facing Main St, was only two hundred total square feet.

When he sat the bag down, the bottles rattled a little. He placed his hand down in the bag to steady them and also to pull one out. There was no mistaking what the bottles contained. They were large and brown. He pulled one close to him and put leverage on the twist top and let the carbon dioxide come out as fast as it wished. He tossed the metal top into the street and then sat back and took several long swallows, remarking to himself how cold the beer still was. When he was finished, he sat back and let his left side sink gently into the arm of the bench while curling his right arm and hand around the bottle, holding it close to his stomach. There were a few vehicles that passed by, and some of the people inside the vehicles gave him confused stares or looks of disgust, maybe pity hidden deep somewhere, but mostly, the people who passed by, even those making a left turn onto News St., disregarded him completely, never noticing him at all. He could have been on fire and it wouldn't have mattered, would not have affected their day until they read something about it later on in the paper, or heard something about it on any number of social media sites. It is also possible that they would never notice Jimmy under any circumstances, never hear anything, and go on in the same way, in the same sense, forever.

One of these cars, a blue car, turned left onto News St.

from Main, then immediately parked in one of several empty spaces that lined the median of the boulevard. She was in her thirties, very stylish, and one would think, regardless of whether or not it was true, that she had spent most of her time getting ready that morning. She wore a dark sort of silk looking floral dress that would have been considered too short to wear if not for the tights that crept down just below her knees. Her flat brown shoes looked like slippers, and all of this darkness was in contrast to her milky white complexion and red lipstick. She and her two children, ten years and five years approximately, crossed over News St, walking toward a coffee shop / kids' indoor playground where many of the local young professionals would go and meet, quaff espressos and let the kids run off the enormous energy that seems to well up from some secret place. Willison was walking behind her children, ushering and pushing them to hurry across News St. when she noticed the large slick bald man sitting on the bench, a sharp reflection of sunlight from a raised brown bottle caused him to stand out. She tilted her head and focused, forgetting she was standing in the middle of the street. Her children were already across and looking back at her.

"Go on in and play. I'll be right in. I'll be right in!" She found herself yelling as the older one took the younger's hand and disappeared into the building, a converted furniture store that had been a converted pharmacy that had been a converted mercantile. As far as she could remember, Willison had never confronted anyone about anything, ever, not a family member, school bully, not a person, animal, or flower. Like her children's energy, it must have been welling up inside her to confront someone, but for her, it was more about helping someone.

An old man in overalls must have better places to suck down cheap beer than the middle of town, in the middle of the Sun, in the middle of the day, she thought. It would not have seemed like much to most people, but for her, "Excuse me, Sir?" were the most dangerous and courageous words she had ever uttered.

"What?" Jimmy answered curtly.

"You're not supposed to do that on the street," she said in a confused tone, as if she were asking a question to the old man. Her courage, she felt like, should be rewarded with compliance, but it was not.

"Are you police?" Jimmy asked quickly.

"No," she said, confused.

"So, you're not gonna move me, right?"

"No, I can't do that. I was just telling you that you can't do that on the street; it's against the law."

"So, you're a lawyer, that's it."

"No sir, I'm not."

"So, you can't *cite* the law *nor* enforce it. Go on away from here. Unless you wanna join me?" he said, smiling and patting his rough hand on the bench. Then, seeing that she was uninterested, offended, maybe afraid, he turned back to a bottle and kept talking. "If it's not Lawyurs it's Poh-lice, or it's Lawyers when it ain't Pohlice. Never there at the same damn time, otherwise they might get their stories straight." He looked back at her again. "An gittin stories straight's bad for business, you catch me?" She stood there, stiff, sweat beginning to form all over her. "I guess not," Jimmy said, turning again.

"You can't do that here," she said again from her perch, a raised place in the sidewalk where a crepe myrtle had popped loose the form. Her small, narrow shoes balanced on the edge like a seesaw, nervously courageous.

"That again?" Jimmy said, this time with a sliver of anger and aggravation in his voice. "Go on away an leave me here. I just wanna be alone."

Several people in the coffee shop had gotten up from their chairs and were looking out the large windows of the store front.

"If you wanted to be alone you-" Jimmy cut her off.

"You wouldn't what? You wouldn't be here in the middle of town?" A pssss sound from the next to the last bottle.

"That's right," Willison said. "And I guess I could go call the Pohhlice." Mocking him. "There's kids around."

"What kids?" Jimmy asked.

"My kids!" She shouted at him.

He took a long draw from the beer, looked down at the gray concrete and spoke sort of slowly. "I reckon there's way worse things for a kid to see." The bottle clanked on the sidewalk as he got up. "I've held this about as long as I can." He walked over to the side of the Doughboy House, manipulated the front of his overalls for at least twenty seconds, and began urinating on one of the several Hawthorne

bushes that made a tiny green moat between red brick and sidewalk.

"This gonna be a regular occurrence Jimmy?" A voice asked from behind.

"Probably. In the service, I could hold it for a day. Every year since seems to bring another heightened sense of urgency."

"Ya drunk yet?" the man asked, his voice sounding much younger than Jimmy's.

“Wait til I'm finished an I'll tell you,” Jimmy said.

“That's enough!” Willison yelled exasperatedly. “Are you going to handle this?” she asked, looking at the other man who had walked over to the brown bag and taken the last bottle out.

“I'll try,” he said, nodding slowly.

“Nuffs a nuff!” Jimmy shouted from behind the Doughboy House. “Let's stand up for Jesus!”

“Pssss” went the last bottle, the amber liquid hit the pavement, the white foam its last surrender. The heat sent steam up from the ground. Jimmy put himself back in, then turned to see as the last of it was leaving a mercurial fog in the air. Then it was gone, and the bottles were clanging in the bag, and Alderman Jones was putting the bag in the back of a small pick-up truck. Jimmy just stood there, kind of foggy himself, wavering sort of as his rough hand rubbed the side of that small building, then he turned back into the sunlight and let it cook his face and his arms while he stumbled to the bench, plopping, forcing himself into it, the wood bending beneath him. He fell into it as if giving up, giving up everything.

ABOUT ATMOSPHERE PRESS

Atmosphere Press is an independent, full-service publisher for excellent books in all genres and for all audiences. Learn more about what we do at atmospherepress.com.

We encourage you to check out some of Atmosphere's latest releases, which are available at Amazon.com and via order from your local bookstore:

Relatively Painless, short stories by Dylan Brody
Nate's New Age, a novel by Michael Hanson
The Bond: How a Mixed Bag of Foster Kids Became a Family for Life, a memoir by A.M. Grotticelli
The Size of the Moon, a novel by E.J. Michaels
The Red Castle, a novel by Noah Verhoeff
American Genes, a novel by Kirby Nielsen
Newer Testaments, a novel by Philip Brunetti
All Things in Time, a novel by Sue Buyer
Hobson's Mischief, a novel by Caitlin Decatur
The Black-Marketeer's Daughter, a novel by Suman Mallick
The Farthing Quest, a novel by Casey Bruce
This Side of Babylon, a novel by James Stoia
Within the Gray, a novel by Jenna Ashlyn
Where No Man Pursueth, a novel by Micheal E. Jimerson
Here's Waldo, a novel by Nick Olson
Tales of Little Egypt, a historical novel by James Gilbert
An Ambiguous Grief, a memoir by Dominique Hunter

ABOUT THE AUTHOR

Scott Roberts is a writer, science teacher, and electrician in semi-rural southern Mississippi where he has lived most of his life. He has an English degree from the University of Southern Mississippi and has taught English and Science (mostly science) at various schools in Mississippi and New England. He lives in Hattiesburg, MS with his wife, two daughters, and a black cat in an old house of heart pine and no insulation. His other works can be found at https://www.beardednarwhalliterary.com/

CPSIA information can be obtained
at www.ICGtesting.com
Printed in the USA
LVHW031320210421
685105LV00005B/118

9 781637 529676